The Wager

To order additional copies, please contact us.
BookSurge, LLC
www.booksurge.com
1-866-308-6235
orders@booksurge.com

ROSEMARY I. PATTERSON, Ph.D.

THE WAGER

A Humorous Novel About Dog Parks, Seniors, and Gambling for Love Later in Life

2005

The Wager

CONTENTS.

To My Daughter Catherine Patterson-sterling, M. A., The Author Of The Self-help Book "Rebuilding Relationships In Addiction" For Her Creative Suggestions For This Book.

To My Good Friend And Fellow Author Edward Michel Bird Whose Latest Mystery Is "Crime Too Perfect" For His Excellent Suggestions And For Listening Patiently As I Plotted The Book.

To The Members Of The West Vancouver Canadian Authors Association Group For Their Invaluable Feedback.

To Margared Hume And The Members Of Her Bkota (Be Kind One To Another) Writing Group For Their Helpful Suggestions To This Manuscript.

To Julie Schmidt And The Ladies Of The Tri Cities Women And Words Writing Group For Laughing At My Early Chapters And Making Suggestions.

CHAPTER 1.
Dog Park.

Even in late fall, Linda 'Canine Lover' Daniels was overcome by the beauty of the area designated as being for the dogs. Although much further north than Hawaii, the area around the designated dog walk reminded her of her vacation trips to Waikiki. The dazzling blue of the sky reflected in the colour on the ocean. She could hear the sound of the waves as they crashed on the shore. The sea wall resembled the one along the shoreline at Waikiki and the mountains were in the same location, behind the high rises built along the shore.

The Dog Park was right where the river flowed into the ocean and the dogs could frolic on the beach, swim in the river, chase each other around trees on grassy knolls and gallop in uninhibited bliss down the concrete walkway. Humans would have to stay alert and leap clear, not the dogs.

It was Linda's sixty-third birthday and the attractive, trim, never married veterinarian chose to spend it along with her dog and human friends at the Dog Park in the hope that company would provide relief from the pain of her two major problems in life. She had never come to terms with her mother's prolonged and traumatic death from colon cancer and for ten years she had been in love with a man who seemed completely oblivious to her subtle and not so subtle attempts to move beyond friendship.

A burst of nervous giggling brought Linda back to her group of dog and human friends spread out over several of the large and comfortable logs on the sand in front of the Dog Park walkway. Linda made sure she had Cleo, her large Doberman, in sight before she tuned into the cause of her friends' hilarity. Cleo had a tendency to take off for long distances after dog acquaintances and then panic if she could not locate her owner visually. A quick glance assured her that Cleo was doing her usual imitation of a submarine and swimming enthusiastically alongside her canine friend, the Wheaton Terrier, Pegasus.

Pegasus was infatuated with Cleo, despite the fact that Cleo could never respond appropriately to his obviously amorous intent. Pegasus would not leave her side and following her usual putdowns of his attempts to seduce her, seemed content to lick her mouth and ears in a series of affectionate slobbers in the hope that sometime in the future Cleo would be more accommodating. Linda managed a short laugh at herself as Pegasus's unrequited love situation somehow reminded the semi-retired vet of her own.

"She can't be serious," Linda thought to herself as the challenge that her wealthy friend Gloria had issued penetrated her brain. "She wants to include Malcolm in the bet this time."

"A new wager," Gloria 'Amorous' Gustafson had said to her five, financially well off friends seated closely together on the logs. They all lived in a beautiful and exclusive gated area on the slopes of a mountain overlooking the ocean.

"Sixty thousand to the one of us who gets Malcolm Brooks into bed by Christmas."

"Good luck!" Linda thought. Her friend Malcolm was a wealthy industrialist who never dated anyone over thirty-five years of age.

"Only one man in the bet. That's too competitive! We need one for each of us." Linda reeled as Esther 'Perky' Goodenough, a power house, older member of the dog walking group and Pegasus's owner, requested adding more men to the bet.

"My God, this is the second time this year they've had this bet. And now they're including Malcolm. I'll just refuse again."

Linda grew further determined to avoid the bet as Gloria agreed with Esther to add more men to the list of eligibles as long as they were from the single, divorced or widowed members of the dog walking club. Gloria also stated that the relationship had to have a sexual component and be maintained for at least a month and that the winner or winners would donate the prize money to a charitable cause of their choosing.

"Are we including you again?" Esther asked.

Linda felt herself losing the effect of the prescription tranquillizer she had taken just before bringing Cleo to the dog park. She recalled that Gloria had won the last four bets of this type. The years did not show on the former leading lady of her movie producer husband's many successful films.

"What if Gloria is successful in getting Malcolm into bed?" Linda thought. "How humiliating. Ten years and I've got absolutely nowhere. Would Gloria succeed in just thirty days or less?"

"I'll be in the bet for sure!"

Linda reeled as the redheaded senior added that it took a lot of brain power to cope with ramifications of an affair.

"You mean it keeps the brain cells moving."

"Exactly! And you all know how much I like a challenge. What about it?"

"Well, some of the single and widowed men do still have their own teeth!"

Linda could not believe her ears as even Virginia 'Prissy' Kelly, a former minister's wife, seemed interested in the wager this time.

"Most of them are still sexually functional," Gloria assured her friends. "Take the one that interests me, Malcolm Brooks, he's a hunk, for someone becoming a Super-senior next month of course."

"Super-Senior!" Linda wondered if that could be true. She was shaking with surprise. Linda recalled again that she had been carrying her crush for close to ten years on Malcolm Brooks, who was one of her most frequent clients. He kept a menagerie of pets up in his immense estate and constantly needed help from Linda.

"Over eighty." Gloria replied, glancing competitively at Linda. Linda started. She had not realised that Malcolm was that old. He looked many years younger.

"Such a thing is possible?" Beatrice 'Plucky' Broughton, a sixty-year-old former university professor demanded.

Linda glanced at Beatrice in disbelief. The slim, attractive lady was slightly paralysed from the car accident that had ended both her husband's life and her University career.

"You should know," Gloria shot back, "being scientific and all. Pharmacology has given those guys their sex lives back."

"What do you mean?" Esther demanded.

"Viagra, Darling. All my beaux use it."

"Well, I did see a recent study that said that sixty-three percent of men over eighty and thirty percent of women over eighty were still sexually active."

"But you're married!" Linda felt glad that the ethics question had been raised as Virginia queried Gloria.

"Gus and I have an agreement, Darling. At our age we figure anything that will keep us from senility is a go."

"Sex keeps you from senility?"

"But of course," Linda grew slightly amused again as Gloria told them that sex was the secret of the fountain of youth.

"Maybe that's what is wrong with me?" Linda thought. "With Malcolm's resistance to my overtures and my resistance to dating others in case he would mind maybe I'm aging too quickly. No wonder I'm afraid I'm becoming addicted to tranquillizers."

Conversation suddenly ceased as a large, greyish, Sheep Dog charged into the centre of the ladies and attempted to lure Gloria's white, Standard Poodle, Gigi, out toward the beach. Gigi pulled desperately at her leash and Virginia's little Boston Bull Dog, Lazarus, started barking loudly and lunging toward the water. Honey 'Y'all' Pratt, a recently retired, Afro-American, Lounge owner from New Orleans grabbed onto her Pit Bull, Bourbon, as he pulled on his leash to get in on the action. Bourbon spit out his cherished, red, phosphorescent ball, pulled out of his collar and joined the large Sheep Dog with his attempts to lure Gigi toward the water.

"Let Gigi go!" Esther advised.

"Gigi's just been to the Voluptuous Canine Grooming Centre. I don't want her fur getting messed up."

"That Sheep Dog is Malcolm Brook's latest dog, Trump."

"Named after Donald Trump, of course!" Linda added, recalling that Malcolm was a wealthy industrialist and worshipped the multimillionaire.

Gloria immediately reached down and freed Gigi. Trump jumped on Gigi and tried to mount her. Gigi used her body to fling him off and headed toward Cleo and Pegasus still swimming in the river mouth. Trump and Bourbon followed in hot pursuit. Linda felt herself smiling a few moments later as four dog heads protruded from the water and the gaggle of Canadian geese that had been paddling around the immediate area shot into the air. Trump, Malcolm Brook's independent minded Sheep Dog, harassed Gigi and Pegasus, the large Wheaton Terrier, frolicked with Cleo.

Bourbon, Honey Pratt's tough, but smallish, Pit Bull, stood glaring at the dogs in the water from the river edge. He apparently did not want to get wet. Linda followed Cleo's cropped ears as the four dogs swam toward the long, narrow sand bar in the centre of the river just before it entered the ocean. The sand bar was only visible when the tide was out. Bourbon finally forced himself into the water as the others moved in the channel toward the bar. He swam rather slowly toward the others with a frown on his face.

"If only Malcolm could be more like his dog." Gloria said plaintively. "He is single, you know."

"I think he is like Trump, but with women half his age and less," Linda supplied. Pain filled her heart as she was reminded of her close friend and client Malcolm's inexplicable pursuit of younger women. He regularly went through two or three a year.

"Malcolm is really a Super-Senior, like me?" Esther's voice betrayed her interest. "He looks years younger."

"He will be eighty in several weeks."

At that instant two Wild Blue Herons who had been standing still in the shallows and waiting for the small fish to return with the tide started flapping frantically. Linda watched the birds with disbelief. The usually still birds took turns displaying their long, bluish-grey, wing feathers and leaping vertically up into the air in a spectacular display.

"Mating behaviour of the Wild Blue Heron," she explained.

"It's an omen," Gloria shouted. "One of us is going to get Malcolm into bed. He's much more like a sixty-year-old."

"I don't know. My late husband would say that you ladies are giving in to temptations of the Devil!"

Linda felt her face grow hot with flushing as Virginia gave them all a look of reproach. Linda realised that Virgie was having second thoughts about the bet. She could feel her own societal conditioning flaring, particularly the overly restrictive childhood she had been subjected to by her wealthy parents. She had been sent to a Catholic, residential school at the age of nine.

"Why?" Gloria challenged. "None of you ladies have a spouse and Malcolm's divorced him decades ago. What's the harm? If one of you ladies can get Malcolm interested in a woman over thirty-five maybe there's a chance for me."

"You're married!"

"I told you, Virgie, that Gus and I have an agreement! And besides, think what sixty thousand would do for your church."

Linda suppressed a laugh. The judgemental look left Virginia's face. She sat silently for over a minute. Linda figured she was trying to process her emotions.

"Well, we have been trying to raise money for a new organ."

"You're in then?"

"Where's the money to come from?"

"I'll put up fifty thousand. The other five of you will be in for the other ten. What about it?"

Linda watched with interest as Gloria put out her hand. Virginia hesitated but then suddenly seized Gloria's hand and shook it.

Esther laughed as Gloria approached.

"Another wager. You know what happened with the last one."

"How was I to know that Steven Purdy was a closet homosexual that just wanted cover for his affairs?"

Gloria reached Linda, put out her hand and the semi-retired veterinarian hesitated. She realised she was not ready to risk her close friendship with Malcolm by directly hitting on him.

"But the Retired Veterinarian Association does need money for research," some part of her mind told her.

"Besides, it's not just sex, y'all know!" Honey Pratt declared as Gloria came up to her. She gave Gloria a "highfive."

Linda listened with interest as Honey, a recent senior, though she looked years younger, and former liquor lounge owner from New Orleans, gave a short talk on relationships. Honey told the astonished ladies that relationships had three components that had to be in place for success. She told them that just good physical sex was not enough, that there had to be a mental bond plus an emotional heart connection as well for a satisfying relationship.

"That's just part of your New Age mumbo jumbo," Virginia argued. You were down in pagan New Orleans for too long."

"For good Tantric sex y'all needs a connection into the mind and the heart as well as the vagina," Honey Pratt insisted.

Linda's mind listened with interest again as Honey told them in her heavy Southern accent that a relationship is one way to get beyond the clutches of the ego. She told them that at least in a relationship a person was going beyond their own boundaries and ego. That, in a relationship, energy was blended from both participants.

"With mind, heart and sex," she insisted "y'all can reach new heights of Spirituality."

"You mean the male energy blending with the female energy?" Linda sighed as she realised she wanted more than anything on this earth to blend her energy with Malcolm's.

"Right on," Honey's face lit up with agreement. "With good sex, a mind and heart connection, y'all can lose all sense of self, even blend in with the All, y'know."

"And the warm afterglow," Linda felt herself remembering her closeness with a former lover while in her twenties. Regretfully he had married another. Tears came to her eyes.

"Unconditional love, Sugar," Honey agreed.

"Then you'll join us this time?" Gloria gave Linda another chance.

"Uh, I don't think so." Linda shook her head. She could not believe she was actually thinking of taking part in the wager.

"My mother's death! I don't think I could handle a relationship right now. It still bothers me?"

"Who said anything about a relationship? That's Honey's hangup. This can be just be a month's roll in the hay. Providing you have proof of some kind of consummation. Just what you need if you ask me."

Linda protested that she was still in a bereavement group.

"That's part of your problem," Gloria retorted. "Sitting with a bunch of weeping people. Do something with the living for a change. Trust me, it's impossible for arousal and depression to occur at the same time. You'll see. Move into the future not the past or at least the present."

"I think Gloria is right," Esther encouraged. "The mind can only concentrate on one thing at a time."

"What about multi-tasking?"

"That's just fast alteration of consciousness," Esther insisted.

Linda felt herself going into a mass of confusing emotions at Gloria's challenge. She was very hesitant to make yet another attempt to lure Malcolm beyond the boundaries of friendship. Just then pictures of the transfer ambulances that had carried her mother to her non-successful treatments flashed into her mind. And the crowd of people undergoing treatments in the Cancer Clinic.

"Every one of them and their relatives hoping they are going to get more time in this world and a lot of them won't. Maybe Gloria is right," Linda felt some part of herself deciding. "It's the same for every one of us. We run out of time unexpectedly and you never know what's around the next corner."

"What have y'all got to lose, Girl?" Honey Pratt insisted.

"Dignity," Linda answered to herself. She had been afraid all these years to express to Malcolm how warm her feelings toward him were.

"What if he actually verbally refuses to become more than a friend." Linda realised she would feel personally humiliated as well as embarrassed. "But if he responded positively her private fantasy could become reality."

Something deep inside her made Linda put out her hand. Gloria took it.

"And you Beatrice?"

Everyone turned to stare at the last member of the ladies dog walking group. The ex-professor walked with the aid of a cane.

"What do you expect me to do?" Beatrice laughed. "Hit some man over the head with my cane?"

"Well, none of our single seniors need to lose any more brain cells. Besides, you are the youngest of the group at sixty. You are just a Junior Senior. You'll think of something."

Linda reeled as Beatrice put out her hand.

"We'll need to figure out which of the single male members of our dog walking club besides Malcolm Brooks are still into sex," Gloria directed. "I think there will be enough of them for all of us."

"Like before," Esther interjected. "We need to eliminate the smokers, heavy boozers, those who have had prostate operations, and those who are in poor health."

Gloria nodded. She told the others that particularly smoking heavily over a number of years finished the sex functioning in men.

"What about Gus?" Esther Goodenough asked.

"He's a possibility," Gloria threw in her eighty-year-old, larger-than-life, movie producer husband. "I told you. We have an agreement."

Gloria pulled out a pen and sheet of paper from her fanny pack.

"OK ladies, give me some names."

Linda jumped up suddenly as a large Rottweiler came charging into the group of ladies. The dog went toward Beatrice Broughton's cane as it leaned against the large log in front of her.

"Christ!" Beatrice screamed as the huge beast grabbed her cane in its powerful jaws and took off toward the water.

Linda realised that the Rottweiler likely thought that the cane was a throw stick. She was used to large dogs of the breed picking up huge pieces of wood, even logs and heavy boulders to play with.

"Do something!" the retired professor's voice was frantic

as the dog stopped, shook the cane at the ladies and then moved toward the water again.

"He wants us to chase him," Linda interpreted. She jumped up and started to chase the huge beast but this only moved him even closer to the water. She moved back toward her friends and the dog approached them again. But this time he shook the cane savagely in the air and pieces of wood came showering at the ladies.

"God, he's destroying my cane."

Linda moved toward the dog again but was interrupted by a sharp whistle from the Dog Park walkway. Linda turned and said a prayer of thanks as the dog's owner blew his whistle one more time and the large Rottweiler dropped to the sand as if he was dead. The cane dropped from his mouth into the sand. The dog's owner walked over to the animal and picked up the cane in his hand.

Six pairs of eyes stared at the man. They realised he was a senior, he had a dog, and he was drop dead gorgeous.

Linda recognized one of her clients from her Veterinarian practice. She wondered if he was a member of the Dog Walking Club.

"Terribly sorry, Ma'am," Linda listened closely to his accent as he was apologising profusely to Bea Broughton. He had a New York sound to his words.

"This cane will never be the same," Bea glared at the man. Linda realised that the others were staring at him too but in admiration. It had occurred to Linda before that the man was a Paul Newman lookalike. Except that he was slightly more muscular.

The man pulled out a pocket knife and cut off the ragged edges from the cane that his dog's large, white teeth had scarred.

"I'll pick you up a new one, Ma'am. Where did you get this one?"

Bea gave him directions to a medical supply store. He promised to pick up a cane that very day, called his dog and started to make his way to the ocean.

"You're one of our new members, aren't you?" Linda grew amused as Gloria charged after him.

"That's right Ma'am. Name's Turk. Turk O'Brien."

Gloria put out her hand and as Linda watched gave the fellow a very warm hug.

"Welcome to the club."

Gloria turned and then moved back to her friends. She waited until he was out of earshot.

"Turk O'Brien ladies! Anyone know if he is single? Or if his prostrate is all right?"

"Mr. Muscles," Linda Daniels told Gloria what she knew about Turk O'Brien. "With a tattoo of a naked lady on his arm. He's single, in good health and doesn't smoke."

"How do you know?"

"He brings in that Rottweiler all the time for routine visits. No trace of booze or tobacco on his breath."

"He has a swagger and a big penis."

"Turk O'Brien?"

"No, his dog. But I suppose the man could have them too."

'What's his dog's name?"

"Dogzilla," Linda supplied.

"I'm going to include him in the bet."

"Dogzilla?"

Gloria laughed loudly.

"No. His owner."

Linda smiled as Gloria gave them all a look.

"He's mine! One of you others can have a shot at Malcolm Brooks."

"Come on ladies, we need some more names."

"Gus Gustafson," Esther volunteered. Gloria gave her a searching look but her husband Gus's name down.

"Frank Simpson," Virginia said.

"Frank! Are you sure? Except for walking Mozart, his Blue Healer, all he does is come out of his mansion on the hill on Sundays and play the organ at the Anglican Church."

"He is a professional organist," Virginia insisted. "And such a handsome man. Doesn't smoke or drink and as long as I've known him he's never been in the hospital for any kind of operation."

"You know, I happened to see him in one of those sex toy and erotic video stores the other day."

Linda stared at Esther in amazement.

"What were you doing in there?" Virginia demanded.

"Never mind!" Esther joked "but be aware that Frank Simpson may be into erotic videos for all we know."

"You must have been mistaken," Linda caught herself laughing as Virginia gave Esther a look of death. "He is a practising Christian you know."

"No matter!" Linda realised that Gloria was ending the argument. "He's likely still sex minded. That should make the task of seducing him easier if anything."

Linda watched with fascination as Gloria put Frank Simpson's name in with Gus in an envelope.

"Tyler Thompson," Honey Pratt volunteered.

Linda started. Tyler Thompson was ninety, had never been married and was very wealthy.

"The Funeral Director," Gloria laughed. "Honey you have a wild imagination hiding somewhere. What about his prostate? Does anyone know?"

"He's one of our Church members as well. As far as I know he's never missed a Sunday by being in the hospital? You know, someone told me he's still a virgin. Lived with his mother all his life until she died at one hundred years old."

"Uh, you've got some of the facts all wrong, Virgie. I could tell you a few things about Tyler Thompson but I'll leave you to figure him out yourself."

"What's his dog's name?"

"Inferno."

"Art Maloney," Esther volunteered.

"The stock broker. He strikes me as being pretty upright. You ladies do like a challenge. But he is a nonsmoker."

"What's his dog's name?"

"Bookkeeper, you know, the Greyhound."

"Malcolm Brooks is still the perfect challenge for you Gloria," Esther laughed.

"Certainly. If that new fellow proves resistant to my charms."

"Malcolm's in, then!" Linda Daniels felt an all too familiar pain in her heart. "What have I done?"

"Ok ladies, a new love affair. You know the candidates. Anyone who appeals to you? Think of a strategy to get to know them better."

CHAPTER 2.
Malcolm Brooks.

Malcolm Brooks and Turk O'Brien arrived at the edge of the beach facing the sand bar in the river at about the same time and took a good look at Malcolm's one year old dog, Trump, harassing a white French poodle. Malcolm could hear the poodle emitting yelps as his large, hyperactive, Sheep Dog lunged at her time after time.

Malcolm yelled at his dog to come and became quite angry as the dog ignored him as he always did.

"Damn!" the tall, wealthy industrialist cursed. He realised that his habitual way of solving problems was not working with Trump. He had thrown money at dog trainers but none of them had successfully conditioned the affectionate but stubborn animal to obey oral commands.

"He's a crime wave on four legs," Malcolm realised as he continued to evaluate the action going on in the water. Gigi was in the lead, yelping frantically, with Trump and Dogzilla hot on her pursuit. The three dogs appeared to be followed closely in the water by a slow-moving Pit Bull. Malcolm watched as things got worse with the arrival of some more of his friends in the dog walking club. Their dogs that were off the leash spotted Trump, Dogzilla, Pegasus, Cleo, Gigi and Bourbon in the river mouth.

Malcolm and Turk watched with increasing anxiety as Frank Simpson's Blue Healer, Mozart, Tyler Thompson's

Rhodesian Ridgeback, Inferno, and Gus's second dog, the Malemute, Inuvik, plunged enthusiastically into the water to join the dogs already cavorting about. Malcolm realised that the dogs were heading straight for Trump, Dogzilla, Bourbon and Gigi.

Gus Gustafson, Gloria's husband, recognized his wife's dog Gigi being pursued and sighed deeply.

"God, Gloria will have a hissy fit. Gigi's just been to the pooch parlour and that ocean water glues her fur together. Not to mention what the sand does when dogs knock her into it."

As Malcolm and the rest of the men followed their progress, Gigi spotted the flotilla of large pooches approaching, emitted more high-pitched, shrieking barks, and headed out to the sand bar in the distance. Trump and Dogzilla splashed after Gigi and the newcomers plunged after Trump with the Pit Bull, Bourbon, following in the rear. Cleo and Pegasus, now exhausted by their long frolic, headed ashore.

Malcolm Brooks became even more alarmed as Gigi, Dogzilla and Trump reached the sand bar and myriads of sea gulls flew up in the air fearing for their lives. He got even more worried as Bookkeeper, Inferno, and Inuvik reached the sand bar moments later and joined Trump and Dogzilla in chasing the large, white poodle round and round in circles on the sand bar. With increasing trepidation Malcolm and Gus noticed the Pit Bull, Bourbon, reach the sand bar shortly after and commence trying to intercept the others by tackling the lead dog every time the dog pack rounded his corner of the sandbar.

"God, Malcolm, call off that dog of yours. Inuvik is very possessive of Gigi. I hope he doesn't get in a fight protecting her."

"I've tried that. Trump never listens."

"Might as well join the ladies." Malcolm sighed as Turk O'Brien, a sixty-nine-year-old retired race car driver, suggested taking a break, pointing at Linda and her friends on the logs near the Dog Park walkway.

"Those dogs won't head in until that poodle of your wife's reaches an exhaustion and heads back."

"You guys go," Malcolm decided in his usual business executive voice. "I'll wait here in case a dog fight breaks out."

"So what are you going to do if that happens?" Malcolm started as Turk challenged his decision. He was not accustomed to others questioning his commands. "Swim out to the sand bar?"

Malcolm looked at the distance to the sand bar and figured he could make it easily. His trainers kept him in excellent physical condition.

"If necessary. It's my dog's fault, I think. He's the one that appears to have started it all."

"That water's frigid, Malcolm," Turk warned.

"Get him fixed!" Gus Gustafson suggested.

"That wouldn't be natural."

"Natural be damned. You're risking a lawsuit if my wife's poodle gets injured. Believe me, Gloria has a temper and a lawyer."

Malcolm groaned. He recalled that Gloria had already threatened him with a lawsuit when his boa constrictor, Raptor, had chased her Siamese cat, Ming, up onto the top of a telephone pole. It had only been the fact that Raptor had just been fed, a Fire Department ladder was available and Gus was able to reason with his wife that had saved the day.

Malcolm motioned the others to go join the ladies and stared out at the sandbar in dismay. Trump and the other dogs were still causing havoc on the sandbar. Malcolm did not even notice as his friends shrugged and moved off to the logs near the pathway.

He spread his expensive, leather jacket on the rock and barnacled encrusted sand and settled down into a resting position to wait for the canines to return.

"Surely, one of those highly paid animal trainers of mind can find a way to cool off Trump. He's got to get more obedient."

"It's not normal to castrate male dogs," Malcolm thought to himself.

A pitiful howl turned Malcolm's thoughts back to the dogs on the sandbar. Trump had Gigi down from the front, Dogzilla was attempting to mount her from behind, and Bookkeeper, Inferno and Mozart were disagreeing about who was next in line. Inuvik and Bourbon were barking and growling fiercely at each other.

"A remote shock device when Trump doesn't listen," Malcolm decided. "To heck with these modern ideas of the owner becoming the Alpha dog himself by picking the animal up and throwing it down on the ground to show who's dominant. Trump just thinks I'm playing when I do that."

More sharp barks, growls and shrieks from Gigi let Malcolm know he was going to have to do something. He could see the white poodle cowering on her back on the sand fending off both Trump and Dogzilla. He took in a deep breath and plunged into the water. Malcolm forced himself to ignore the frigid water and plunged in further. He managed to get his arms and legs to coordinate in his usual powerful swimming stroke. Within a couple of minutes he reached the sandbar.

Malcolm staggered onto the sand, stepped in between Trump and Gigi and pulled the determined Sheep Dog off the now thoroughly muddy and frantic poodle. Gigi ran for the water.

"Down," Malcolm yelled. Trump ignored him and tried to follow Gigi. Malcolm picked up the dog, threw him down and attempted to hold him. He cursed as Trump immediately broke free and ran off in pursuit of Gigi. Unfortunately so did the other dogs. Malcolm had just managed to stand up when he felt the sharp collision of the Blue Healer, Mozart, the Pitbull, Bourbon, and the Malemute, Inuvik, as they crashed into both of his knees. He went down with a bang. The wealthy industrialist felt the pain in his knees drowned out as the huge Rottweiler, Dogzilla, and the Rhodesian Ridgeback, Inferno, stormed over him grinding his head into the sand and barnacles on the sandbar. Malcolm felt himself scream involuntarily and panicked as he realised he could not see properly. He staggered onto his feet and took several halting steps into the water hoping to wash the sand and debris from his eyes. Unfortunately Malcolm felt his injured right knee snap, his legs give out from under him and within seconds he realised he was submersed in the water without being able to see.

Malcolm thrashed about in the cold water trying to free the sand from his eyes.

"Christ, I hope I'm not moving into deeper water. I can't tell which way I'm going." Malcolm felt his breathing became even more agitated as the pain and frigid water took their toll. He panicked further as he still could not manage to see which way was toward shore.

"Lord, I hope I'm not heading out to sea."

For the first time Malcolm thought about his upcoming birthday. He would be eighty, though personal trainers kept him in the shape of a sixty-year-old or younger. The thought really depressed him.

"It's the start of these decades," he said to himself as he

started to suppress the knowledge that there was no way he was going to make it back to shore by himself without help. "You just get used to the decade you've reached and then suddenly you're at the next one."

CHAPTER 3.
Turk O'Brien.

Hell, those dogs have knocked Malcolm down," Turk exclaimed as he saw Malcolm being run over by several dogs. "There's a crime wave out on that sand bar." But as Trump and Gigi reached the members of the dog walking club in a hail of sand, water and barks he turned his attention to the problem at hand. Turk realised that his own dog, Dogzilla, was galloping toward them on the beach. He blew his whistle at his dog and became quite angry at Malcolm as Gigi cowered behind Gloria and Trump kept lunging at her.

"Malcolm really should do something about that dog." Then he worried further as Inuvik and Inferno caught up and both made a lunge at Trump.

"Do something," Turk's mind registered that Gloria was screaming, as Gigi was clutching onto her and whining piteously.

He noticed the woman with the cane stand up, move close to Gigi and hold her damaged cane up high in the air. Turk realised that the spunky little woman meant business. He grabbed onto Trump, pulled him away from Gloria but the large Sheep Dog broke free. Cursing, Turk seized his own dog and dragged Dogzilla over to one of the metal and wood benches along the walkway, put the end of his leash through the handle and attached the dog to the bench. He watched with approval as Gus then grabbed Inuvik, leashed him and attached him to a neighbouring bench. He noticed Art Maloney grab his Greyhound, Bookkeeper, slip on his leash and then hold him. Turk frowned as he noticed that Trump was still thundering around causing havoc and that all the dogs were barking fiercely at each other. He stared back at the ocean and realised there was an even worse problem happening. Malcolm was even further out to sea.

"Malcolm is in big trouble out there," he advised. "And the ocean is swallowing up his jacket. The tide's coming in."

Turk watched as the dog club members rounded up the last of their freed dogs. He approved of the way most of the dogs obeyed. As Turk kept a close eye on the scene, Tyler Thompson's Rhodesian Ridgeback, Inferno, sat as ordered. His own dog, Dogzilla, cowered and stopped trying to pull free of the bench as Turk threatened him with obscene curses. He watched Frank Simpson's Blue Healer, Mozart, collapse to the ground with exhaustion. As Trump approached again and made for Gigi he made sure he grabbed the dog securely this time. Within a minute the former race car driver had the Sheep Dog securely attached to Dogzilla's bench with another leash.

"That's the way to handle these dogs," Turk noted with approval as Art Maloney's Greyhound, Bookkeeper became immobile as the stockbroker placed an electric collar around his neck. He watched Honey Pratt grab an exhausted Bourbon when he finally arrived, take him over to another bench and fasten him to it. He smiled with approval as Linda Daniels told Cleo to freeze and she obeyed as she always did. He noted that Angus, Bea Broughton's Pomeranian was in her arms cowering and Virginia Kelly's Boston Bull Dog, Lazarus, was hiding under a log.

"Damn, Malcolm is still swimming out to sea even though the tide is coming in," he shouted as he anxiously scanned the ocean again. "My God, he's missed the edge of the final sandbar."

He and the other walking members started shouting Malcolm's name frantically. Turk and the other men left any unattached canines to the ladies and moved out toward the rapidly advancing water's edge.

Back in the ocean, the shouting penetrated through to Malcolm Brooks in the midst of his frantic paddling. Some part of his brain registered that the noise was coming from another direction than the one he was heading in.

"My God, I am swimming the wrong way," he groaned. Malcolm turned his body in the direction of the howling and shouts. His body was telling him that it was exhausted and his one good knee was becoming harder and harder to move. Malcolm realised he had better go over on his back and rest for a while if he wanted to regain his energy. He managed to roll over, assumed as much of a float position as his knees would allow and tried to ignore the waves crashing over his head. Malcolm felt movement and realised that the tide was now coming in and it was moving him toward the shore.

"He's managed to turn around," Gus told the others as the men stared out at the ocean at Malcolm and the incoming tide. The water was starting to swirl around Malcolm's jacket.

"God, the tides coming in fast. We've got to get that jacket out of there."

"To Hell with the jacket. What about Malcolm?"

"He'll float in."

"He's been in that water for quite some time. Might be getting hypo-thermic."

Turk muttered some obscene curses, rushed down the

now disappearing beach and moved into the water. He swam rapidly toward Malcolm. The others watched Turks right arm rhythmically appearing out of the water.

The muscular, Paul Newman lookalike, reached Malcolm just as the wake generated by a freighter moving through the ocean past the sandbar crashed over his head and he sank beneath the waves. Turks dived down, grabbed hold of Malcolm from behind and brought him to the surface. He held Malcolm's head above the waves with one arm and pounded him on the back with the other. Malcolm coughed and sputtered as the water retched out of his lungs. The pain in every part of his body faded as he lost consciousness. The frigid water had finally numbed him completely.

Turk pushed his powerful body to swim rapidly to shore towing Malcolm behind him. As he reached dry land Turk slung Malcolm over his back and deposited him in amongst his friends and their dogs on the soft sand around the logs near the walkway. Trump howled and tried to break free from the bench he was tied to. Malcolm was ominously still and silent.

"It's hypothermia," Linda stated, her mind frantic with worry about Malcolm.

"I've called the paramedics," Gloria held up her cell phone. Linda bent over Malcolm and tried for a pulse in his wrist.

"He's still breathing but the pulse is faint."

Turk grabbed hold of Gus's Malemute, Inuvik, and freed him from the bench. He dragged the dog over to Malcolm and motioned for him to lie down. The dog spread himself over Malcolm's chest and lower body.

"Inuvik will warm the bastard up," he explained.

"Good idea." Linda removed a scarf from her around her throat and motioned for Esther to give her the bottle of water she was carrying in a pouch. Esther passed the water over.

Linda poured some of the water onto the scarf and cleaned off the sand and blood from Malcolm's face and nose. She lifted his eyelids and poured some of the water into his eyes. Sand and particles of barnacles washed out. Malcolm groaned.

By the time the siren signalled the arrival of the paramedics Malcolm was starting to reach consciousness again.

"What's he saying?" Gus Gustafson demanded.

"I think he's calling Trump."

"Don't worry about Trump, Malcolm," Gloria assured him. "Gus will take him home with Gigi and Inuvik."

"Thanks," Gus groaned.

Malcolm seemed to be able to use his eyes as the paramedics arrived. The eyes were open as the emergency workers checked out his vital signs and transferred him onto a stretcher.

"One of us should go with him," Frank Simpson insisted.

"I'll go if someone will look after Cleo," Linda felt anxiety forming as she took in Malcolm's condition. Tyler Thompson signalled he would take care of Cleo. Linda followed Malcolm into the ambulance.

Inside the ambulance Linda found herself seated next to Malcolm's stretcher. He groaned and she placed her hand on his. His eyes opened wide and he seemed to be staring at her as if he recognized her.

"Blanche?" he questioned. Linda went into shock.

"No Malcolm. It's Linda. Linda Daniels."

A look of great disappointment filled Malcolm's face. He slipped into unconsciousness again.

"God," Linda realised. "He's still missing his divorced wife and it's been twenty years, they tell me. And all those young women. Maybe, he's getting even for Blanche leaving him."

Linda felt her heartbeat increase as she stared around

the ambulance. It reminded her of all her mothers' transfer ambulances. She had accompanied her to all her cancer treatments.

"I wonder if now I'm going to lose my best friend?" The ambulances always reminded her of the impermanence of life.

"My tranquillizers," Linda reached into her jacket pocket and pulled one of her prescription pills out of its case. "I really should stop using these, they're becoming addictive," she warned herself again.

CHAPTER 4.
Musical Chairs.

Lying in his hospital bed Malcolm Brooks decided he must look like one of those disaster photos of a skier who has gone over a cliff and has broken every bone in his body. He stared at his right leg hanging in a cast and a strap, his right arm held up by a triangular bandage and at the tube slowly dripping some kind of liquid into his left arm. He felt terrible and wished that part of his entourage would clear out of the room. He was surrounded by his latest girlfriend Monica, employees, personal trainers, members of the dog walking club and his nephew and heir, Lorne Brooks. He wondered why Gloria Gustafson kept visiting him and hanging around for so long each time. He also wondered about the myriads of flowers filling his room from many of the female members of the dog walking club.

"This is what happened when Blanche left me," he recalled. "My God, they must be after me again. But what could have caused the frenzy this time. I thought I had finally convinced the ladies, especially Gloria, that I was only interested in young things."

Malcolm glanced at Gloria Gustafson and Esther Goodenough looking expectantly at him from chairs in his room. He decided to give them a message and motioned Monica over to his side. He grasped her right hand with his left and told her how glad he was to see her.

"Maybe that will do it?" he thought hopefully.

Monica looked shocked.

"I didn't know you cared so much Malcolm. You've never told me so."

Monica kissed him warmly on the lips. Despite the bandages Malcolm felt himself responding sexually to the voluptuous young woman leaning over him and kissing him passionately.

"God, not here," he thought. Fortunately Monica removed herself from his side as three additional ladies came into the room. They stared at Monica with astonished looks.

"I better not do that again," Malcolm thought as Monica blew him a kiss from across the room. "Monica might get the idea she's more than a temporary plaything."

Malcolm recognised some more of the single ladies of the dog walking group.

"So Sugar, how are y'all feeling today?"

Malcolm groaned. He was a secretive and private person and the act of someone he barely knew calling him "Sugar," particularly someone he was not in the midst of pursuing, in front of a group of his employees, his girlfriend, other friends and dog walking club members left him mortified.

"Well, you do look a lot like the Michelin Tire Man with all those bandages."

Malcolm groaned again. Gloria had confirmed his worst fears.

"He's not that bad." Malcolm felt slightly better as Linda Daniels challenged Gloria.

"Linda's not like the others," Malcolm was surprised to find himself thinking. Since Blanche had left him, he had been extremely defensive with female members of the dog walking club. "Linda's always been a good friend. Always responds so quickly when one of my animals needs attention."

"Thanks Linda," Malcolm told her forgetting to censor the warm tone in his voice.

"Who are you?" Monica demanded, jealous of Malcolm talking to another member of the opposite sex in a warm voice.

"My veterinarian, Dr. Linda Daniels. This is my girlfriend, Monica Mason, Linda."

"Oh, you're the lady that takes care of Malcolm's animals."

Linda realised that Monica had written her off as an animal attendant. She wondered what Malcolm saw in such a bimbo.

"And what do you do, Monica?" Linda felt herself giving into her own jealousy.

"Modelling. I'm with the Montgomery agency."

"I should have known," Linda thought, suddenly feeling even more jealous of Monica's youth and perfect figure.

"This is not like me at all," she realised. "My crush on Malcolm is bringing out my shadow side or something."

The room suddenly turned into absolute chaos as Gus Gustafson came into the room with Trump and his own dog, Inuvik. The large, young, Sheep Dog charged over to Malcolm on the bed knocking Monica over in the process. She crashed to the floor with a crash and Inuvik licked her face.

"My contact lenses," Monica screamed. "The dog's licked them out."

Linda suppressed a laugh as the young woman felt desperately around for her missing contact lenses. It was obvious she could not see very well at all without them. Turk O'Brien picked up Monica from the floor just as Trump got past her and leaped onto Malcolm on the bed. Malcolm felt sharp pains shooting through every part of his body. He screamed.

Turk grabbed the wiggling dog and lifted it off of Malcolm.

Malcolm noticed even more people coming into the room as Monica gave up the search for her contact lenses, crashed into the wall on the way out and abruptly left.

"I'll see you later, Darling," she shouted on her way out. "When we can be alone."

Malcolm groaned. It was the first time Monica had called him Darling.

"It's so hard to disengage them when they think they have a chance to become a wife," he thought.

Malcolm tried to reach for the buzzer for a nurse to limit the number of visitors but Inuvik chose that moment to lick him on the face and more visitors came into the room.

"At least they're male," Malcolm glanced past the Malemute at the men and recognized some more of his friends from the dog walking group. He gave a big sigh of relief as Linda came over to the bed and pulled Inuvik away.

"She's not like the others," Malcolm decided again. The appraisal left him shocked. He was moved to rebuild his now automatic defences against women around his ex-wife's age as he realised he was finding Linda attractive as well as helpful.

"It must be the near death experience. I've never felt like that about Linda before." Malcolm banished thoughts of the attractive and intelligent veterinarian out of his head.

Linda stared at the tall, slightly portly industrialist covered in bandages.

"Why do I find him so attractive?" she wondered.

"Turk's the one who swam out and brought you to shore," Gus Gustafson told Malcolm. "You owe him big time."

Malcolm put out his hand to the towering man who was keeping Trump restrained on the floor.

"I can't thank you enough," he exclaimed. "You saved my life."

"Weren't nothing. Someone else would have done it if I hadn't."

"You were very brave," one of the ladies told Turk. Malcolm realised the lady with the cane was Beatrice Broughton, an old friend of Blanche's from the University.

"Gus and Bea are right," Malcolm spoke up. "I remember swallowing a huge wave that crashed over my head just as you turned up."

"Anybody would of done it."

"I owe you big time. Anytime you need a return favour think of me."

"Thanks, I'll remember that."

"You've got to do something about that dog of yours, Malcolm," Gus insisted. "He's been driving Gigi nuts. I had to shut him in the garage before Inuvik killed him."

"I'll take him," Turk volunteered. "He and Dogzilla have an understanding."

"Or I can take him." Beatrice Broughton advised. "My back yard is fenced and my Pomeranian, Angus, and Trump get along fine as long as no female dog is present."

Malcolm stared at the large, tabooed man and the slight, former university professor with surprise. Tears came into his eyes. He never wanted to bother people and had few if any close acquaintances. He was overcome that two relative strangers were offering to help out.

"We'll take turns with the dog, Ms. Broughton. I'll take him tomorrow and you can have him for the rest of today."

Bea nodded and Malcolm thanked them both.

"Hopefully I'll be out of here soon. But the leg is cracked in three places. They're planning what to do about it."

He stared at the pile of sheepdog hairs on his bandages left by Trump and became aware of the new pain in his groin.

"God, I hope he didn't crack anything down there."

"My car is down in the parking area, Mr. O'Brien. Perhaps you could put Trump in it. Please call me Bea."

"If you'll call me Turk. I'll come down and place the dog in the car and then follow you home to get him into your yard. You sure you can deal with a dog this size?"

"He'll be all right thanks, Turk."

Malcolm, Linda and the others watched in amazement as the former race car driver got a hold of Trump's leash and accompanied Bea Broughton out the door. He was at least a foot taller than her.

Linda noticed that Gloria had her mouth open in amazement.

"Bea beat Gloria to the starting gate," she thought.

Malcolm stared at his nephew Lorne as he moved deliberately through the room and stood in front of Linda Daniels.

"Malcolm, who is this attractive woman?"

Malcolm noticed Lorne looking at Linda's empty left-hand ring finger.

"My veterinarian, Dr. Linda Daniels," Malcolm growled.

"Linda, this is my nephew and one of my vice-presidents, Lorne Brooks."

Linda stared at Malcolm's nephew. He looked a lot like a younger version of Malcolm. Linda figured he was around her own age. The man shook her hand warmly.

"Would you have time for lunch, Dr. Daniels? I'd like to confer with you about one of my pets?"

Malcolm stared at his nephew in astonishment. He was quite sure Lorne did not have any pets. To his amazement a stab of jealousy struck him as Lorne moved off with Linda Daniels into one of the corners of the room. When the two of them disappeared out the door a growl came to his lips. He remembered that Lorne was single. He had never married and was quite a womanizer.

He felt a growing anger at his nephew and main heir as his employees, a doctor, and remaining members of the dog walking club descended on him.

Ten minutes later in a Japanese restaurant in the heart of the city Linda found herself admiring the view and the man seated with her. The restaurant was surrounded by wooden walkways spanning water-filled pools complete with multicolored fish. Malcolm's nephew seemed charming and a slimmer, younger version of Malcolm himself. Linda noticed that his speaking voice was quite different. Malcolm was all business. Lorne had a much more intellectual voice.

"You're concerned about a pet?" Linda was used to inquiries from friends and casual acquaintances about their animals.

Lorne Brooks shook his head.

"Forgive me, Linda, for that ruse. Actually it's you I'm interested in. I'd like to take you to the symphony next Friday? Kiri Te Kanawa will be the guest performer. How about it?"

"You don't have a significant other?" Linda was quite taken with Malcolm's nephew. "It's probably his resemblance to Malcolm," she realised.

"No, not at the moment."

"Well, thank you Lorne. I've wanted to hear Kiri in concert for a long time."

The waiter arrived with the food and Linda enjoyed her lunch immensely as Malcolm's nephew turned on his considerable charm. Toward the end of the meal Lorne became more serious.

"You don't mind if I ask you a question about Malcolm do you?"

"Malcolm?" Linda was taken aback.

"Yes, I take it you've known my uncle for years?"

"I've been his vet for ten years."

"I'll be frank. I'm sure you're used to confidential discussions."

Linda nodded.

"Good, you see I want to know if you've noticed any changes in Malcolm's personality?"

"Changes?" Linda was not pleased with Lorne's question? It was not concern about Malcolm she was detecting in his voice. She began to wish she had not agreed to attend the concert with Lorne.

"Yes, you see the Board of Directors is concerned about some of Malcolm's business decisions lately. His judgement has been off and the running around he does with young women draws a lot of bad publicity for the company."

"Bad business decisions?" Linda felt herself growing increasingly irritated at Lorne Brooks insinuations. And she certainly was not going to discuss Malcolm's taste for young women or his dating practices with anyone.

"Heavy investment in his horse racing empire. You know he had a lot riding on the Kentucky Derby. His horse, Star Walker, was a favourite but didn't finish in the final three. Malcolm has spent a small fortune on facilities, trainers and even jockeys to bring him this far."

"I wouldn't know about good or bad decisions in horse racing," Linda tried to evade the man's questioning. "Or in business, for that matter."

"We're concerned about Malcolm's age. You know he will be eighty in a few weeks. Have you witnessed anything that might indicate senility, memory loss, or deterioration in mental functioning?"

Linda felt herself recoiling from Malcolm's nephew. She regretted even more having agreed to attend the next symphony concert.

"He's certainly not concerned with Malcolm's well being," she concluded.

"Malcolm hasn't changed one iota over the last ten years," she testified. "He's always been concerned about his animals, gives them the very best of care, and makes wise decisions about their health."

Lorne did not seem pleased at all by her answers.

"What about this last incident? Swimming out into frigid water to separate two dogs doesn't seem very wise to me."

"Malcolm is the most responsible person I know in all relations with his friends," Linda testified. "He thought he was to blame by bringing an untrained dog to the dog park and was just doing what he thought it was his responsibility to do."

Fortunately the waiter interrupted the conversation with the bill. Linda was about to go back on her agreement to attend the concert with Lorne. However Lorne sensed her displeasure and switched back to talking about the local arts and culture scene, a topic that he sensed Linda was very interested in.

"Some desert, Linda, or another cup of coffee?"

Linda glanced at her watch, put down her knife and fork and stood up.

"I'm sorry, I'm going to be late for an appointment. Thank you for the lunch."

"I'll pick you up on Friday at 6:30 p.m."

"Thanks." Linda decided to give Malcolm's nephew another chance. "Perhaps he is just concerned about Malcolm," she decided.

Linda accepted Lorne Brook's quick kiss on her cheek and left the area.

"She's too loyal to Malcolm," Lorne decided. "Maybe I'd be better talking to that latest girlfriend of his, Monica Mason, I think her name is. A no-brainer if there ever was one. The Montgomery Agency, I think she said she's with."

Lorne pulled out his cell phone and got the number of her modelling agency. He gave the name of a fictitious magazine to the modelling agency, mentioned Monica Mason, a possible article and procured her cell phone number.

"Monica?" he questioned as Malcolm's current girlfriend answered his ring.

"This is Lorne Brooks, Malcolm's nephew. Would you like to attend the world championship boxing match with me next Saturday? I've managed to get two tickets for it."

Monica screamed.

"The championship. However did you get tickets?"

"A scalper." Lorne realised it was going to cost him plenty to procure the tickets.

He hung up the phone in a very positive mood.

"One of those ladies, I'm sure, can give me the dirt on Malcolm I need," he sighed. "I'm going to be sixty-three years old soon and it's about time I got my chance to be the President of Brooks Enterprises."

CHAPTER 5.
Bea and Turk.

Bea Broughton smiled to herself as Turk O'Brien's flashy, high speed sports car followed her classic Acura into her driveway.

"I'm in the lead," she thought. "I've managed to lure one of the eligible singles to my house. The spinal cord injury research fund can really use the money from the wager."

Bea opened her attached garage with her remote and drove into it. She waited as Turk jumped out of his car and opened the door of her car for her.

"My Goodness. That good looking man is a gentleman."

Bea moved out from behind her steering wheel and using her cane walked over and opened the door to the back yard. Her Pomeranian, Angus, rushed into it as he always did. The next door neighbour's large grey and white, Persian cat, Mistletoe, had a habit of sunning itself on the playground that Bea kept in her backyard for her grandchildren and Angus always expected to find the cat there.

A loud barking barrage let Bea know that Mistletoe was indeed present. She smiled as Turk let Trump and Dogzilla out of the backseat and they bolted for the open door to the back yard to find out the source of the barking. A sharp yelp let Bea know that one of the canines had encountered Mistletoe's sharp claws. The large cat was not one to run from a threat.

"The neighbour's cat," Bea explained. "We'll let the animals sort themselves out, shall we?"

"Good idea!"

A hail of barks, hisses and loud meows let Bea and Turk know that the animals were indeed doing just that.

"Would you care for a cool drink, Turk?" Bea invited. She enjoyed the man's surprised look.

"Thanks, I would."

Turk followed Bea through a side door and into her modern kitchen. He noted that it was neat as a pin and he marvelled at the number of pots and pans and other culinary objects that were present hanging on the walls and on shelves.

"You love to cook?"

"I used to. Seems problematic now, though, with my husband gone.'

"Too much food?"

"Yes. Even if I freeze it I never seem to want to eat it."

"I understand. I use restaurants a lot, myself."

Bea motioned Turk to come into her living room. He entered and marvelled again at the tasteful antique furniture and art objects neatly arranged in the living/dining area. Bea's three university degrees were in frames on the wall. He felt oddly out of place amongst the display of degrees, fine china and artifacts from around the world.

"This is a very educated and sophisticated lady," he concluded, feeling intimidated. "She's a beaut, too."

He glanced down at the coffee table and did a double take at what he saw. A sales brochure for a luxury care home was open on the table. Turk felt himself reacting with anger. The brochure pushed one of his buttons.

"Why is that there?" he demanded.

"My son and daughter-in-law, I'm afraid. They think the house is too much for me and want me to sell it and move into an assisted care facility."

"You're much too alive, young and vibrant for that if you ask me."

Turk sat down rather hesitantly on one of the antique chairs. It creaked a bit. Bea looked a bit apprehensive.

"Do relax on that lounger, Turk. I'm afraid these old chairs might not be up to a man of your size."

Turk moved to a comfortable lounger by the television set.

"Wine, or Ale?"

Turk was surprised that Bea had his favourite drink on hand.

"Ale would be great, thanks."

Turk watched as Bea went into the kitchen area and returned with a bottle of ale and a glass mug. He poured the amber liquid into the mug and took a sip with appreciation. To his surprise Bea came back with a mug of ale herself.

"You like ale?"

"Uh, I imagine it goes well on a hot day."

"Does one of your children have your Power of Attorney?"

Bea started in surprise.

"Why yes," she admitted, "my son John, but why do you ask?"

"Take it back!" Turk decided to be honest.

"Whatever for?"

"A friend was slightly paralysed. Like you. Nothing serious. From a mild stroke. Her daughter got a Power of Attorney drawn up and before you know it the next time she had a fainting spell from the heat my friend was shoved into a nursing home against her will."

Bea looked aghast as Turk continued to tell her about his unfortunate friend. He claimed that the stress of trying to get out of the nursing home caused another, stronger stroke and the poor woman was kept confined to her bed for several years until her son and daughter convinced a judge she was brain dead and her life support was cut off. He told Bea that when the actual will was probated little remained as care facility fees and unauthorized loans to her daughter had used up all the money.

"That's horrible." Turk noted that Bea was not saying that such a thing could not happen in her case.

"Take my advice."

"Thank you. I'll consider it."

"Would you like to have dinner with me?" Turk decided to ask Bea out. He was rather lonely and the former professor reminded him a lot of his friend who had wound up in the nursing home.

"You don't have a significant other?"

Turk smiled. "No, I'm divorced," he explained. "Long hours working on my race cars. And travel all over the country. Got home one day and my wife was gone. Took me a while to get over it. Found someone else but the same thing happened with her."

"Did you ever tell either one of them that you missed them or ask them to come back?"

"No," Turk laughed ruefully. "Truth of the matter is that I decided that 'man's best friend' was enough company for a man like me and I've had a series of Rottweilers ever since. Dogzilla is number five."

For some reason Bea felt sorry for Turk O'Brien. "He's never learned to communicate with a woman," she concluded. "Maybe she could teach him." Bea thought of Gloria Gustafson's wager. "Funny if I won it instead of one of those able-bodied women."

"There's a good restaurant down at Tynehurst Point. Overlooking the ocean. Staff are dog friendly. We could take the dogs. There are tables out front in the glassed-in porch and places to tie dogs up nearby. Don't hurry with your ale, though."

"Sounds good to me." Bea ignored Turk's advice and drank down the ale rapidly. Minutes later Bea realised she was feeling a little tizzy as Turk opened the door of his sports car to seat her in the passenger seat. Bea wondered what the neighbours would think as she moved out of the driveway in Turk's flaming red, custom built Porsche. Dogzilla and Trump were manipulating for room on the back leather seat. Little Angus was dominating the open window.

"Hope the neighbours don't tell John about this," Bea thought of her problems with her son's control issues since her husband's death.

"He won't even let me manage my stock options myself. It's like I'm spending his money or something."

Bea felt a strange thrill as Turk accelerated quickly down the winding, scenic, curvy road along the ocean. The ale helped her to relax quickly as his big hands guided the steering wheel with great precision.

"What an adventure," Bea told herself as she noticed a powerful attraction to Turk's physical presence. "Maybe I'm not yet ready for the 'Down Memory Lane Care Home' as my son insists." Bea started to feel quite rebellious.

Bea stared at Turk's handsome face and his large arm muscles with a strange appreciation growing in her mind.

"His penetrating, blue eyes do something to me," she acknowledged.

"After all he is a racing car driver," she thought. "Something odd happened to me the moment he sat in my living room. I seemed to have changed somehow. First time I ever drank the ale I keep on hand for my son. I even liked it."

An hour later Bea started as Turk brought his Porsche to a stop in the parking lot of the Tynehurst Ocean Restaurant. Turk had been playing crossover cowboy music and Bea had somehow lost herself in the melody, rhythm and words. "You're always on my mind," Bea laughed at the appropriateness of Willy Nelson's song. "He never called her, never sent her flowers, but she was always on his mind. Poor woman. Sounds like Turk's wives."

If the staff thought something was rather incongruous at the contrast of the large T-shirt and jeans wearing, tabooed man with the Rottweiler plus the Sheep Dog and the Fortrel suited lady with the Pomeranian they never showed it. The hostess recognized Turk as a big tipper and seated Bea and the former race car driver at a table on the porch where they would have a full view of the sunset. The waiter even allowed Dogzilla, Trump and Angus to be attached to the base of the table. He brought each of the dogs a bowl of water and a large dog biscuit.

"Drinks?" he queried.

"A large ale and your biggest T-Bone steak," Turk ordered.

"And the lady?"

"A Lava Flow," Bea decided, feeling adventurous as she looked at the cocktail menu. "And I'll have a T-Bone steak as well."

"Three burgers for the dogs," added Turk.

"Certainly, Sir."

"You're partial to Hawaii, I take it?"

"How did you know that?"

"Your cocktail."

"I do love the islands. Such natural beauty and the underwater scene; beautiful, multicolored fish and corals."

"You scuba-dive?"

"Used to," Turk could feel the sadness in Bea's voice. "But I suppose I could probably manage to at least snorkel now. As long as my son wasn't present. He would never let me even enter the ocean, I'm sure."

Turk gave her a lecture about the importance of exercise in maintaining muscle strength and mobility. He told her how he had been seriously injured in a car crash but managed to almost fully regain his strength by exercise and certain herbal products.

"We'll go to Hawaii and I'll have you scuba diving again in no time," he promised.

Bea suddenly thought again of her son, John, and her daughter-in-law, Orphelia? "I wonder how they would take that news?" she laughed to herself. Turk was giving her new hope that she could live a normal life. Bea suddenly realised that Tyneburst was one of John and Orphelia's favourite restaurants. She felt momentary sadness and a strange anger descend on her again at her son's unexpected insistence on her moving to a care facility.

"I'm really not ready to let go of my house," Bea decided. "And that assisted care home won't take animals, I'm sure. Whatever would I do without Angus? Perhaps this man is right and I should revoke my 'Power of Attorney," Bea found herself worrying. "It must be Orphelia's influence but John doesn't seem to be disagreeing with her at all."

The waiter arrived with the drinks and lit the candle on the table just as the sun set in a dramatic fashion. Bea could swear that a blinding flash of green had occurred just as the sun had sunk behind the horizon. The sky lit up with the downed sun's reflection illuminating the clouds in the sky. It was as if an artist had splashed a series of red and oranges across the sky in a dazzling fashion.

"Just for us," Turk O'Brien proclaimed. He lifted his ale glass and Bea clunked her Lava Flow cocktail glass against his.

"That sunset was an omen. They're always like that in Hawaii. To the rest of the fall," Turk announced. Bea felt a shiver up her back as he gave her full eye contact.

"This man is such a romantic," Bea thought in surprise. She downed her Lava Flow much too quickly.

"Another?" Turk asked as the waiter arrived with the steaks. Bea nodded.

"Two refills!" Turk ordered.

"What's happening to me?" Bea wondered as his voice caused her body to quiver with excitement. She plunged her knife into the largest steak she had ever seen. "And I'm a vegetarian," she thought. Bea realised that something from deep in her subconscious was coming to the surface. She found herself eating the steak with unexpected gusto.

"Repressed sexuality," her mind suddenly informed her. Bea strangely remembered that while her husband, Thomas, had demanded per functionary sex regularly, he had never provided the foreplay that would have heightened her appreciation of the act. She reached suddenly for her second Lava Flow.

"Maybe this man is different," Bea felt some part of her mind hoping.

As Bea downed her second Lava Flow, her feelings of deep pleasure suddenly vanished as she realised a familiar voice was addressing her in anger.

"Mother, whatever are you doing here with this man?"

Bea turned and realised with shock that her son John was standing slightly beside her and was addressing her in a very angry tone. His wife Orphelia was glaring at her two empty Lava Flow glasses.

"Oh, Turk, allow me to introduce you to my son John and his wife Orphelia. This is Turk O'Brien.

Turk O'Brien stood up and offered his hand to Bea's son. John Broughton just ignored it.

"Turk? What kind of name is that?"

Bea realised that Orphelia was glaring now at the large tattoo of a naked lady on Turk O'Brien's arm.

The table suddenly lurched sideways as Dogzilla heard the anger in John Broughton's voice and moved, trying to get in front of Turk. He growled menacingly. Trump, now Dogzilla's close buddy, joined him in a sharp growl and the table moved closer to John Broughton dragging little Angus whose anxious barking filled the porch.

"What the Hell are you doing here with this man and his savage dogs?" John Broughton challenged his mother. Bea was completely mortified.

"John, you're being very rude to a dear friend of mine!"

"You're coming home with me, right now!"

John seized his mother's arm, pulled her up from her chair and started to drag her out to the parking lot. Dogzilla lunged, pulled over the table and snapped his leash. He went for Bea's son.

"Freeze," Turk O'Brien commanded as plates, glasses and cutlery shot into the air, landed on the floor and smashed into a thousand pieces. Dogzilla dropped to the floor and froze on the spot. Trump was barking savagely and the table was moving around. Angus was covered in coconut milk from the remains of Bea's lava flow and howled pitifully.

"Back off!" Turk shoved John Broughton away from his mother.

"Police!" Orphelia shouted at the top of her voice.

Bea felt tremendous embarrassment flowing through her. People in the main area of the restaurant were now staring at them through the glass wall.

"A problem, Sir?" the manager of the restaurant spoke to Turk.

"Call the police," Orphelia demanded. "That vicious dog is threatening my husband."

The restaurant manager looked at Dogzilla sitting absolutely still and silent on the floor.

"Doesn't look like it to me."

"We were just leaving," Turk advised the manager. "Sorry about this mess. This should cover the bill and the damage."

Turk handed the manager several large bills, freed Trump and Angus from the table, put his arm around Bea and moved the shaking woman toward the parking lot.

"Dogzilla, come."

The large Rottweiler followed but kept his eyes on John Broughton.

"Mother, don't you dare go off with that man," John Broughton yelled at Bea's retreating back. She turned.

"I don't know when I've been so ashamed of you John!"

Bea allowed Turk to escort her out of the restaurant. The manager stepped in front of John Broughton when he tried to follow.

By the time Turk drove back into Bea's driveway the rich food and the two cocktails had loosened Bea's usually strong moral conditioning. The dreadful scene made her feel extremely rebellious toward her son. When what Bea was now viewing as a sexy senior sensed receptivity and pulled her close against his powerful torso she offered no resistance. Following a deeply passionate kiss, Turk opened the garage door with Bea's remote, placed all three dogs in the backyard, returned to the car and carried an almost unconscious Bea up through her kitchen door, through the living room and onto her comfortable and luxuriously adorned bed in her bedroom. Turk did not turn on the light as he undressed both Bea and himself. He used the light of the full moon shining through the window to guide him to sensual areas in a display of foreplay that had Bea in ecstasy. Through a haze of sensuality she was experiencing sensations in areas she had not even known existed. By the time Turk allowed himself to reach completion Bea's sex life had been transformed forever.

The next morning Bea awoke with the worst hangover she had ever experienced. She staggered out to the kitchen, swallowed several headache pills and found Turk cooking her breakfast in the kitchen.

"All my love," he told her, planting a kiss on her forehead. Bea's heart fired up and an unfamiliar warmness settled around her heart.

"He's so gorgeous and so romantic," she thought.

Her positive moment was shattered, however, as Angus suddenly went into a barking fit at the front door. Bea peered out her window.

"Oh, God!" she muttered. "It's John and Orphelia. I forgot they were coming this morning to take me on a tour of that Assisted Care Home."

"I'll handle them for you," Turk offered.

"No, I'll have to make peace somehow. For the sake of my grandchildren. Please go!"

From her tone of voice Turk realised that it was important for Bea to take care of the matter. He nodded.

"I'll take Trump. Call me when you want me to return him." Turk placed one of his cards into Bea's purse on the counter and headed for the back door blowing a kiss before he disappeared. Bea rushed to throw on some clothes as her son and daughter-in-law moved toward the front door.

"Who the Devil is that?" John Broughton asked moments later as his wife and as he could not help but notice a car with a Rottweiler's head sticking out the back window moving out of Bea's driveway.

"Damn! Didn't get a good look at him. I think it was that fellow with the odd name from the restaurant."

"I told you your mother is brain damaged from that stroke!"

"Don't be ridiculous, probably a delivery man."

"At 8:00 a.m. in the morning. Your mother is having an affair, John."

"You're jumping to conclusions."

"Look how long it's taking her to open this door. I'm telling you we have a serious problem here. If she marries that man her will is invalidated."

Orphelia launched into a discussion of the state's community property laws. By the time she was through John had become as highly anxious about his mother's behaviour and the consequent danger to his inheritance rights as Orphelia.

"I'm going to speed up our arrangement with the Director of the Care Home," Orphelia told John. "Divert your mother and I'll use my cell phone."

"Who was that man leaving your driveway, Mother?" John demanded as Bea finally opened the front door. "Is that the man from the restaurant yesterday?"

"None of your business!" Bea marched into the kitchen.

Orphelia gave him an "I told you so," look and flipped open her cell phone.

"Proceed today as we planned in several weeks time," she instructed the care home director. "Yes, speed up the action. Today! We may not get her back again."

"Turk is right," Bea thought as John interrogated her angrily in the kitchen. "I really should revoke my 'Power of Attorney.'"

CHAPTER 6.
Honey and Tyler.

Turk O'Brien stared hard toward the parking lot of the Dog Park. His eyes were searching for Bea Broughton and Angus. It was half an hour past the usual meeting time and Bea was nowhere to be seen. Turk became more anxious that Bea had not returned the messages he had left for several days about dropping off Trump as expected.

"Wonder if she minded getting so close so fast?" he wondered. "Or maybe she's caved into her son's demands because of the grandchildren." Turk felt quite a bit of pain in his heart about such a possibility. The pain merged with some of the intense emotion Turk had experienced with the rejections from his two wives. Nausea struck him in his stomach.

"I'll have none of that Shit again," Turk vowed. "I'm not going to call Bea again until she calls me."

He released Trump and Dogzilla and sprinted after his friends who had gone ahead with their animals.

Up ahead Honey Pratt was having a talk with Tyler Thompson, the local Funeral Director, who had intercepted her as she walked Bourbon. His Rhodesian Ridgeback, Inferno, and her Pit Bull, Bourbon, made a strange pair as they ambled together, just in front of their masters. Honey, Tyler, Inferno and Bourbon were several hundred yards behind the other Dog Walking Club members. As they came to a grassy knoll with trees and a ravine behind it Inferno suddenly went down on his front paws facing Bourbon and barked.

"Isn't that cute, Sugar?" Honey said to Tyler as Bourbon took up Inferno's challenge and roared off as fast as his shorter legs would allow up to a grassy knoll and then into the ravine behind it. The Rhodesian Ridgeback roared after him and very quickly caught up, rolled the Pit Bull over in his charge, grabbed Bourbon's cherished red ball, from which Bourbon was inseparable, and then shot behind some trees in the ravine. The sturdy Pit Bull picked himself up and used his nose to follow Inferno behind the trees. In a few seconds the sound of barking and growling reached Tyler and Honey.

"This man is my best chance to win the wager," Honey said to herself as she gave in and joined the well-dressed, distinguished looking, ninety years old in conversation. "This old boy has been flirting with me since I joined the Dog Walking group. Nothing gross, just winks and compliments."

"Y'all never have married?" she queried.

"Why settle for one when you can have the pick of the crop any time?"

Tyler's answer startled Honey. She had the same philosophy herself. Ever since the love of her life had vanished out of her life when she was twenty-five years old leaving her with three kids less than six to raise.

"This old boy is loaded with self-confidence," Honey decided, as Tyler Thompson put his arm around her shoulders, stopped her in the middle of the concrete walkway, and gave her a sensuous kiss. He seemed oblivious to the stares of onlookers. A sensuous pat to her seat made Honey come back to the present as Bourbon and Inferno came roaring back. Honey noted that Bourbon had his ball back. Tyler moved them all in the direction of the other walkers.

"Getting him to bed is going to be easy," Honey interpreted Tyler's behaviour. "But I bet hanging onto him for as long a month isn't."

"Y'know, I've always been interested in the mortuary business. The range of coffins and funeral accessories is amazing. How do y'all get people to buy those expensive coffins."

"Come over to my Chapel this afternoon," Tyler invited. "I've got a large service scheduled for four o'clock. I'll give you a personal tour of the graveyard and showroom afterwards."

"You're on Sugar," Honey agreed. She approved of the way Tyler disengaged himself from her as Turk O'Brien's Rottweiler, Dogzilla, and Malcolm Brook's dog, Trump, came pounding down the pavement. Honey noted the Funeral Director staring at Turk himself as he approached jogging from the rear.

"He doesn't like gossip," Honey gave a sigh of thanks. "At least amongst people who know him." Honey surveyed the wealthy funeral director openly as he chatted with Turk O'Brien.

"He's lost none of his height," Honey decided, "weighs as much as he should, no more, and that cute little, neatly trimmed beard conceals any jowls if they exist. Not bad for an aging Caucasian."

Even though she usually preferred men of colour for possible significant others, Honey decided to explore a possible short-term relationship with Tyler Thompson.

"Sixty thousand would provide at least ten Afro-American scholarships for college, I could add some myself, and maybe that old boy could be hit on for a few more, maybe in his will."

Honey checked her watch. "Eleven-twenty, plenty of time to change and find something suitable for that funeral," she thought.

Honey whistled for Bourbon, now in the ocean next to the beach with Inferno, Dogzilla and Trump. He swam in obediently and trotted up after recovering his red, phosphorescent ball on the sand. She gave him a treat and quickly attached his leash. Tyler and Turk stared at her in surprise.

"Sorry y'all, got an appointment, have to leave early" she winked discreetly at Tyler. He smiled knowingly back. Honey moved Bourbon in the direction of the parking lot. Bourbon whined and pulled at his leash as they moved away from his canine friends.

"Sorry Bourbon. Don't worry, I'll make it up to y'all." Honey reached for

another treat from her fanny pack.

Later at the funeral chapel, Honey regretted missing most of the morning dog walking session but she was taking advantage of the scheduled funeral to attempt to attract the attention of the never married Funeral Director. She was glad that Tyler was another of Gloria's designated eligible members of the Seniors Dog Walking Club. Honey looked around the impressive chapel until she located her person of interest.

"He's my best chance of winning that wager," Honey reminded herself as she surveyed the dignified, still handsome man keeping his eye on all aspects of the elaborate funeral being conducted for one of the members of the District Chamber of Commerce. She noticed him smiling at her across the chapel. Honey gave him a wave. He waved back.

Linda Daniels, who had agreed to accompany Honey to the funeral noticed their interaction. "So that's the reason she wanted to come to this funeral," Linda realised. "I guess I should try and do something about Gloria's wager, myself, but I don't feel up to the challenge. She realised that her long time crush on Malcolm Brooks and Gloria's bet were causing severe emotional turmoil.

"What if I make a direct pass at him and he refuses. I'll lose him as a friend for sure."

Linda went over in her mind about her daily visits to Malcolm in the hospital. She acknowledged that they were having great conversations about things of interest to her like animals and their health. Malcolm was particularly interested in the health of race horses and she had done some research on the matter for him. Linda also assured him that she was keeping a close eye on his menagerie of pets up at his estate. Linda told him that his Howler monkeys, named Loud and Even Louder, his Boa Constrictor, Raptor, his Green Tree Python, Squeeze, his black Jaguar, Diego, his Cassowary Bird from New Guinea named Razor, and his large Pyrannas, Vicious and Reprehensible, which he kept in a specially built fish tank in his living room, were all doing well. Linda sensed how important these matters were to Malcolm.

" But he's not really showing any sign of being attracted to me, just glad of the company to pass time I think."

Linda thought about her date coming up with Malcolm's nephew Lorne.

"Maybe he is a possibility," she felt some part of her mind speculating. "After all he does look a lot like Malcolm and we're both interested in the art and culture events going on in the community."

"Anyone who is anybody in the business community is at this funeral," Linda whispered to Honey. The Chapel was full of the bankers, lawyers, politicians and business people who had held the deceased, Joseph Connor, the local Cab company owner, in high esteem.

Linda laughed as she thought about the long procession of cabs she had witnessed on the way in. The procession had followed the extra-long, black, luxurious, hearse carrying the deceased the short distance from the mortuary to the funeral chapel. Joseph Connor's wife and now owner of his cab company had paid every one of their cab drivers to wear their uniforms and to polish their bright orange cabs to take part in the procession in keeping with her husband's wishes. Linda pondered on how marriages and funerals were such displays of wealth and celebrated with considerable elaboration by well off people.

"It's like ancient Egypt," she mused. "People must think that the elaborate coffins and memorials are going to impress people in the next world," she wondered. "Or maybe they're just for the survivors to impress their relatives and friends?"

"Y'know, I bet there isn't a cab available to be had anywhere," Honey chuckled.

"There must be chaos at the airport," Linda agreed, " Joseph Connor had a monopoly on the cab contract there."

"I really appreciate y'all coming with me today. Some of these folks still don't like a person of colour taking part in high society events, even funerals."

"Nowadays?" Linda's voice expressed her disbelief in Honey's implications.

"Y'all take a good look at those graves out there, Girl? When was the last time that a person of colour was buried in them?"

Linda started. She had been looking at the gravestones, as Joseph Connor's epitaph had attracted her attention. His newly dug grave awaiting his state-of-the-art coffin was adorned with a gravestone with a picture of one of his cabs on it and the name of his company. She realised that Honey was right. Every name that Linda had recognized had belonged to a white person of the community. There had not even been a Chinese or Japanese name despite the abundance of ethnic homesteaders and their descendants dating back from when the area had first been homesteaded. Linda's face flushed as she realised for the first time that people of colour must be buried somewhere else.

"Oh my God," Linda muttered. "Segregation even in death."

"Exactly, Girl."

Honey and Linda, along with their fellow funeral participants grew silent as Tyler's sonorous voice started the service and he introduced the local minister of the Anglican church. The minister then asked Tyler to do the Eulogy. Honey realised that the elderly Funeral Director who looked and sounded years younger than his age still had his brain cells fully intact. He never missed a word, made a clever observation about cab drivers as important transportation facilitators and had every eye in the audience wet from his references to the deceased never-failing kindness and sense of humour. At the end of the service Honey and Linda filed out of the chapel with the others to witness the casket being lowered into the newly dug grave.

As the minister said the well-known words of dust to dust and ashes to ashes Linda recalled her intense pain at her mother's funeral less than two years before. "What's it really all about?" she wondered again. "Maybe there isn't anything more than dust to dust and ashes to ashes." Tears welled up in the semi-retired veterinarian's eyes. She dabbed at them discreetly.

"There's no real death, Sugar," Angie realised Honey was trying to help her. "The real you, the part that we'all call soul or mind or 'I am' is just freed from the restrictions of the body, y'know."

As Linda was trying to process Honey's advice she noticed Tyler working his way through the crowd toward them.

"I must be going," Linda told Honey as she sensed her friend's anxiety. "I promised Malcolm Brooks I'd come and bring him some of the latest information on optimizing health for race horses. He's having troubles with his racing stable."

"Y'all have the hots for him, don't you sugar?"

Linda freaked and then laughed. She suddenly realised that Honey was telling her why she found Malcolm so attractive. "It's his virility," she acknowledged. "He's been turning me on for years but I mistook the feeling for love."

"Is it all that obvious?"

"Just to a trained eye, Sugar," Honey reassured her.

"It's so painful. Unrequited love. I hope you're right, that it's just unrequited sex."

"Don't make any difference, Sugar. I you ask me they're both just as painful."

"I've had a crush on that man for over ten years. I don't understand it."

"Y'know, I think you are making a big mistake putting that man on a pedestal and dreaming about him all this time. Y'all living in fantasy, Girl."

"What should I do then?"

"Let your illusions go, Sugar. Avoid all contact with the man."

"I know he's got a lot of emotional baggage but he is a good friend and client."

"Baggage, that man's got a whole lifetime of unresolved issues, and the money it takes to play dating games with attractive, young bimbos like that latest girlfriend."

"But he needs someone to take care of him and his animals."

Honey Pratt groaned.

"Y'all must be a Venus In Pisces, Girl. They're either

forever rescuing helpless things in need or living their lives in romantic fantasy."

Linda felt strong nausea in her stomach from Honey Pratt's assessment. It hit home sharply. She reached for another of her tranquillizer pills.

"A Venus in Pisces. An Astrologer friend mentioned I had that placement once, I think. How would I know for sure?"

"Just get your Horoscope done. It'll show you the position of all your planets."

"I think I'll go do that. Look, good luck with Tyler."

"Thanks Sugar, I'm going to need it. By the way, watch out for that young girlfriend of that Malcolm Dude. Think she's a Scorpio and they'all don't like rivals. She was eyeing y'all pretty closely in that hospital room until that Inuvik dog knocked out her contact lenses. Think she could tell that Malcolm speaks rather warmly, for him, to y'all."

"Malcolm speaks to me rather warmly?"

Honey laughed. She realised that Linda had only heard the words about Malcolm speaking to her warmly.

"Y'alls got it bad all right. Look Sugar. Pay attention to my words. Watch out for that Monica. Attracted to the man's money, I think. Just watch your back if y'all know what I mean."

"This is all too complicated for me."

Linda moved off with the crowd, her mind and emotions whirling. Thoughts of Malcolm, mixed up with thoughts of his nephew Lorne, mixed up with thoughts that Malcolm already had a girlfriend, mixed up with thoughts that Malcolm spoke to her warmly, mixed up with thoughts that she spent too much time living in fantasy, mixed up with the thought that she was using too many tranquillizers.

Within seconds Honey Pratt realised that Tyler Thompson

was violating her personal space. His bigger than life presence was much too close to her body. The Funeral Director took her hand is his large one and held it warmly as he kissed it sensuously.

"Won't you join me, Ms. Pratt? For the reception. It's just a short stroll through the cemetery. On the other side of the hedge."

"Why thank y'all, Mr. Thompson. But please call me Honey." She took Tyler's offered arm and felt him pull her against his body as he led her in the direction of the reception area. Somehow his tall, trim body seemed extremely comfortable against hers.

"Sex appeal, at his age," Honey recognized.

"Now Honey, don't even think of leaving after the reception," Tyler winked knowingly as they reached the reception area. "Remember I'm going to give you a personal tour of the behind the scene's areas." Honey stared at him in amazement as he left her side to personally oversee the details of the reception.

Honey moved about enjoying a fine wine and the luxurious spread of hors d'oeuvres but was conscious of both unfriendly glances and people going out of their way to assure her how welcome she was in their community.

"I thought it would be better up here in the North," Honey mused. "But it's just different not better. Half the people wish you were living somewhere else and the other half are going overboard to let you know they're not bigots." Honey avoided talking to Joseph Connor's widow. She wasn't sure which category the cab owner's wife was in.

It was a relief when the reception was over. As the guests left the area Tyler approached.

"I wonder what category he's in," Honey felt herself growing really cynical.

"Ready for the tour, Honey?" Tyler Thompson gave her full eye contact and a friendly smile. Honey felt reassured.

Tyler put his arm too comfortably around her again and led her into his showroom.

Honey stared at him in fascination as he explained the pros and cons of every model of coffins and memorials in the room. She could not believe it when Tyler gave her the sales pitch for titanium coffins for two, coming with waterproofing, earthquake proofing, a full corner in the cemetery complete with a tree and a large rock with the names engraved on it. Plus perpetual upkeep and gardening.

"Y'all really think there's going to be a resurrection and bodies are going to come out of these coffins to join Jesus?"

"Well actually I don't, Honey," Tyler laughed. "I think everything ceases when the brain dies. But you'd be surprised how many wealthy Christians buy this model."

Tyler pointed at two polished tubes connected to cylinders. Honey laughed as Tyler suggested that since she was obviously a nonbeliever she might be interested in the titanium ashes holder that would be stored in the earth for perpetuity.

"Following cremation, of course."

"Actually Sugar, I want my ashes to be spread on the ocean. That way even the particles of matter get returned fast for recycling."

Tyler smiled warmly again and resumed their tour of his showroom. Honey was blown away by the variety and cost of many of the items.

"Well Sugar, what do y'all plan to do when you die?"

"I'm not going soon," Tyler Thompson joked. "My mother lived to one hundred. Maybe by the time I'm one hundred and thirty."

Honey followed Tyler up a set of stairs to the top floor.

When they stepped out she realised with surprise that he had taken her to his living quarters. The upstairs apartment was surprisingly avant garde with futuristic furniture and uncluttered space. Inferno, Tyler's Rhodesian Ridgeback, greeted his master with enthusiasm. He gave the dog a massage along the ridge on his back and the animal responded with much affection.

"That dog means a lot to him," Honey thought.

"At last we're alone," Tyler sighed. To Honey's surprise Tyler didn't initiate intimate relations. He moved her into his living room and seated her on his futuristic chesterfield but he stayed standing himself.

"Would you care for a Bourbon?"

"How do you know my favourite drink is Bourbon?"

"The name of your dog."

Honey blushed. "That old boy doesn't miss a thing," she thought.

"Thanks, Sugar, a Bourbon sounds real good." Tyler moved to the panelled wall, pressed something and a hidden cabinet revolved to the front. Honey looked around Tyler's apartment. Everything was modern, futuristic, state-of-the-art, and in excellent taste. She watched as the Funeral Director poured out two generous Bourbons, added some ice and water, returned to the chesterfield, handed Honey hers and sat down himself on the chesterfield but not close to her.

Honey paid attention to his body language. She realised with puzzlement that it was not suggestive of further intimacy; in fact it looked like he was being quite defensive. The arm closest to her was across his chest almost in a protective manner.

"That old boy is a master of seduction," Honey hypothesized with surprise. "He's trying to get me to make the first move." Honey revised her earlier estimation that it would be easy to get Tyler Thompson to bed.

"Only if I suggest it," Honey realised. "I bet that old boy would rationalize that I'm a person of low morals and he's just teaching me a lesson as he drops me after like a hot potato."

Inferno, the Rhodesian Ridgeback, laid his body down at Tyler's feet and looked at him expectantly. Tyler placed his Bourbon on an end table and gave the dog another deep massage. The dog smiled and whimpered appreciatively.

"I wouldn't mind the old boy doing that to me," Honey realised.

She took a sip of her Bourbon. She recognized her favourite brand.

"My favourite Bourbon. How did you know about it?"

"I'm a fan of all kinds of Jazz. Visit New Orleans often."

"I like jazz, myself. But Dixieland is my favourite."

Tyler Thompson immediately got up and went over to a modern piece of furniture. He pressed something and a CD player appeared. Within seconds Dixieland jazz filled the room. He sat back down and Honey realised he was wearing her favourite eue de cologne. A strange feeling struck her in her heart.

"My God, this old boy is twanging my heart strings, I must be losing it completely."

Honey felt the sudden onset of the panic that hit her when she was in danger of falling for a member of the opposite sex. For all her recommendations of the perfect relationship leading to higher Spirituality to the female dog walking members Honey rarely practised what she preached. Two intense but failed relationships in recent years had left her with an unwillingness to fall under the spell of certain members of the opposite sex, particularly ones for which she felt a strong sexual attraction. Honey felt something inside her telling her to get out of this man's presence fast. She recognized deep attraction at first sight, and there was no way she wanted to allow the vulnerability produced by intense attraction.

"How come no one of colour is buried in this cemetery?" Honey felt herself demanding. She realised she was blowing it for the wager but some part of herself wanted to create an argument that would allow her to get out of the intimate situation fast.

Tyler Thompson looked startled.

"Actually," he managed, "I was going to try and do something about that, Honey. Do you want to take out a burial agreement? For you or someone else in your family?"

"Then this cemetery is segregated."

"It has been, I'm sorry to say. Common practice in the cemetery business. The other two large cemeteries in this area are still segregated as well. But if you wish you or some member of your family can do something about it."

Honey realised that Tyler was somehow putting the ball back into her area of the court. She felt her temper flare at his challenge.

"The empty family plot next to the cab company owner. I'll take it."

Honey realised that she was shaking with rage and that she was almost yelling. She realised that she was anticipating Tyler saying that such a thing was impossible.

Tyler's dog seemed to sense her rage and got up from the floor, went in between his master and Honey and growled.

"Down Inferno!" Tyler ordered. The dog obeyed instantly.

"I'll make the arrangements, Ms. Pratt," Tyler Thompson rose from the chesterfield. "I can see that I've distressed you. My apologies."

"If you wouldn't mind coming back down to the office? I'll have you sign a contract and drive you home?"

Honey realised that she had been dismissed. She could feel her face heating with all kinds of emotions.

"What an experience," Honey choked back all the responses she wanted to shout. She managed to pull herself together enough to nod brusquely at Tyler and move toward the door of the hallway leading down to his showroom.

"Jesus, I've bought an expensive funeral plot," Honey muttered to herself a short time later as Tyler drove her toward her residence in his fancy Italian sports car. "And I'm ending the segregation of a cemetery, or at least when I or a member of my family dies. This man is a master manipulator. And much too attractive as well."

Honey sighed as she realised in her mind that she was physically still much too close to the man. His physical presence, the excellent way he handled his sports car, and the Dixieland jazz he was playing on the car's CD player were turning her on. She made sure she got out of his car fast in front of her house before he could give her another of his sensuous kisses.

Tyler blew her a kiss as she turned to look at him just before going in the front door.

"He knows I'm attracted to him," Honey realised with a sinking feeling in her stomach, "despite my anger outburst." She shut the door with a bang.

"So much for winning Gloria's wager. I had better make sure I don't get alone with that old boy again. I'm not sure I can resist him for long. I'm going to wind up begging him for sex if I don't, I'm sure."

"Charlotte, I've purchased a family plot in the cemetery for us," she told her astonished daughter who lived with her as she entered the front door.

"Mom, who was that man that dropped you off and blew a kiss at you? Y'all not thinking of dating a Caucasian are you? He looked white."

"Course not Charlotte. That's the local funeral director. I just bought a funeral plot."

"Thank goodness! I was worried I'd have to try and explain why you were dating a Caucasian to all my friends back in New Orleans."

"Don't have to worry about that, Girl! I have no intention of ever speaking to that man again!"

"Why did y'all buy a funeral plot, then? I thought y'all believed in cremation."

"Uh, just to end the practice of segregation in big cemeteries up here, Girl."

CHAPTER 7.
Malcolm and Linda.

It was 9:00 a.m. as the dog walking group met two weeks later to allow their pets to swim in the ocean mouth off the dog park entrance. Not many members were present as there was a light rain falling.

"For God's sake, Linda, Malcolm is back." Gus Gustafson pointed toward the entrance to the Dog Walking section of the park.

The wealthy industrialist could be seen at the start of the dog section scanning the crowd of dog owners looking like he was watching for his old friends from the Seniors Dog Walking Club. He was using crutches and moving slowly for Malcolm.

Linda Daniels was shocked. Malcolm had said he was going to be released but was going directly to Kentucky to make some changes in his horse racing facilities. He had told her that the Kentucky Derby had been a big disappointment for him months ago as his horse "Starwalker" had failed to place despite being the favourite. Linda could tell from her recent hospital visits that Malcolm was grumpy and discontent. She realised from their discussions that he was looking back at the last thirty years of his life and wondering if he had made a bad choice to invest in his widespread horse racing and training empire.

Linda felt herself comparing Malcolm and his nephew Lorne. To her surprise she had enjoyed her date with Lorne at the local symphony. Kiri Te Kanawa had been magnificent and Lorne seemed to enjoy the performance as much as she did. Linda realised that Lorne was much more informed about cultural and art matters in the community than Malcolm. He had been the perfect gentleman, dropping her off at her house immediately after they had an ending drink. The only thing that was bothering her about accepting another invitation from him was the questions he kept asking about Malcolm.

"Does Malcolm forget things?" he had asked and "Is Malcolm ever late for meetings or not show up at all?" "Are your bills to him paid on time?" "Can Malcolm always remember names that he should remember?" "Had she ever noticed any deterioration in Malcolm's cognitive functioning?" " Did Malcolm ever drink to excess in her presence?"

Reviewing the questions in her mind Linda realised that Lorne had almost been checking off questions from a mental functioning checklist. Linda realised that she had done the right thing by refusing to accept Lorne's invitation to another upcoming symphony concert.

"He's just using me to try and dig up some dirt on Malcolm," she realised with a stab of pain. Her thoughts turned back to Malcolm's approach on crutches across the sand and rocks.

Malcolm Brooks hesitated as he came to the start of the dog walking park. He ignored Tyler Thompson, who seemed to be trying to get Honey Pratt to talk to him, looked out to the ocean and spotted Gus Gustafson talking to Linda Daniels on the sandy area exposed from the ocean when the tide was completely out. Malcolm had come to find Trump. He wanted to take him with him to Kentucky. He was missing the only source of unconditional love in his life.

"I wonder if Trump is going to be another failure?"

Malcolm mused. Trump had received the attention of several of Malcolm's animal trainers but his stubborn nature had proved extremely resistant. Trump would come, heel, sit, fetch and roll over but only at his own pace (erratic) and provided that something more interesting had not already captured his attention.

"Sort of like Monica," Malcolm realised with a slight laugh, thinking of how fast she had gone back to directing all her attention to her modelling career with him in the hospital.

"Call when you get out of this boring place," Monica had requested.

"After I get rid of the crutches," Malcolm sighed. He did not feel up to making love while using crutches.

"I guess I had better try walking out on the sand to where Gus and Linda are," Malcolm decided to ignore his doctor's advice to take it easy and stay on smooth, flat surfaces for quite some time. He moved onto the slippery sand, barnacles and rocks, ignored the instability, and moved slowly on his crutches toward his friends.

"They'll know where Trump is."

"Hello Gus," Malcolm said as he reached his old friend.

Gus Gustafson greeted him with a hug. "Nice to have you out of the hospital."

Malcolm shrugged. Linda Daniels stared at Malcolm. As always, he was extremely well dressed.

"You look better without the hospital gown," she teased. Malcolm gave her a slight smile. He started to move in her direction but when Linda glanced beyond him she gasped as she realised that Malcolm's dog Trump had spotted his owner from the walkway and was heading down the beach toward him at lightning speed.

"Look out Malcolm!" Linda shouted but it was too late. Trump crashed into his owner with a sickening bang and Malcolm went flying once again. Trump jumped on his sprawled master and lavishly licked him on the face.

Gus Gustafson grabbed hold of the impulsive dog and hauled him off Malcolm. Linda could see that Malcolm's right leg was jutting out at an awkward angle. Turk O'Brien arrived on the scene, yelled some obscene curses at Trump, leashed him and pulled him out of reach of Malcolm.

Malcolm was conscious but was uttering a series of curses himself in between moans. Linda bent down and gingerly examined Malcolm's right leg. He groaned loudly.

"Looks like it's broken in one place," she told Gus. He reached for his cell phone and punched in 911.

"The paramedics will be right here," he told Malcolm who looked like he was making a mighty effort not to scream.

Linda took off her jacket and placed it under Malcolm's head. He placed one of his hands appreciatively on her right hand. It looked like he was making an effort to say something.

"Don't try to talk," Linda ordered.

Tyler Thompson and Honey Pratt came rushing out and a crowd of people was gathering around Malcolm.

"We could try and carry him to the walkway," Tyler offered.

"No, don't move him," Linda ordered. "We need to get his leg stabilized first."

By the time the paramedics arrived with a stretcher Malcolm's face was a pasty white. Linda held Malcolm's shoulders as one of the paramedics lost no time in straightening Malcolm's leg and applying a blow up splint around it. Sweat poured off Malcolm's face. He let out a massive groan as the leg was moved and he lost consciousness.

"Isn't this the same old guy we picked up off the beach a few weeks ago?"

"It is," Linda told them.

"Must have a death wish," the paramedics joked as they wheeled Malcolm back toward the ambulance.

"I'll come with you," Gus Gustafson told Linda. "Turk will you watch the dogs?"

The big man nodded.

Half an hour later Gloria arrived at the start of the Dog Walking Park and bumped into Tyler and Honey as they were leaving?"

"Have you seen Gus and the dogs?"

"Gus went with Linda Daniels to the hospital. The dogs are with Turk O'Brien. Toward the bridge."

"To the hospital? What happened?"

"Trump crashed into Malcolm again. This time it looks like Malcolm's got a broken leg."

"That dog! I don't know why Malcolm hasn't got rid of him. My God. I had better find Turk and the dogs."

Tyler and Honey watched Gloria head off at full speed down the walkway.

Tyler was taking advantage of the fact that he had managed to engage Honey in conversation again. He could feel her prickly attitude toward him lessen somewhat. They were suddenly interrupted as Bourbon, Honey's Pitbull, and Inferno, Tyler's Rhodesian Ridgeback, had another disagreement over Bourbon's cherished, red, phosphorescent ball. Conversation ceased as both dogs ran up to Tyler and Honey. Inferno had the bright red ball in his mouth and he was obviously seeking help to fend off Bourbon who was growling and snarling, demanding his ball back.

Tyler pulled the ball out of Inferno's mouth and threw it down the beach. Both dogs shot after it.

Honey felt herself feeling an odd mixture of pleasure and fear again. She realised she was in a sweat from contact with Tyler's physical presence for so long a time.

"That old boy is far too attractive, I shouldn't be speaking to him again," Honey tried to regain some semblance of her normal coolness toward men she felt herself strongly drawn to.

"There's a Dixieland Jazz concert at the Patriot next Saturday."

Would you allow me to escort you there?"

His invitation did something to Honey.

"Subconscious longings," she decided. "He's tapping into desire energy from long ago."

"Saturday at six o'clock. I'll pick you up." Tyler took her silence as assent as Gloria and Turk joined them with an assortment of dogs including Dogzilla, Trump, Inuvik and Gigi.

Honey tried to say "No" but felt her head nod affirmatively. She felt greatly relieved as Tyler kept an acceptable distance between them as they ambled off with the others and the dogs toward the parking lot.

"I'm going to have to take a cold shower when I get home," the former lounge owner told herself. "And before he turns up to take me to the concert."

Honey's disturbed mind told her that she was vacillating between eager anticipation of Tyler's attentions and fear of the abandonment that had so often occurred in the past as attractive men had only been interested in short-term affairs.

"If anyone is emotionally unavailable, I bet it's he," Honey's mind told her. "But it's only a month to Christmas. The bet just says a month. Surely I can hold on to him that long."

Honey reminded herself that the college fund could make good use of the money.

Back at her house Honey was tempted to call Tyler and cancel their date. She confided her problem to her daughter, Charlotte, who lived with her and quickly wished she had not.

"How could you think of dating a Caucasian, Mother? You must be losing it."

Honey told her daughter that Tyler's race was not the problem but that his considerable sex appeal was.

"Who is this man, anyway?"

Honey told her that he was the local Funeral Director, that he was all of ninety years old and had never been married.

"Ninety years old! What are you doing, mother, rescuing a senior from some seniors centre like you rescued Bourbon from the dog pound? You've got to stop being so compassionate."

Honey protested that Tyler was not a rescue senior. She tried to get Charlotte to understand that every time she had felt extreme attraction to a man it had ended badly. Charlotte kept missing the main point.

"White, ninety years old, a funeral director, never been married," y'all have lost your marbles! I'm going to get a one way ticket for you to New Orleans before you do something y'all regret for the rest of your life. What could y'all possibly have in common with this man?"

"Tyler loves dogs, New Orleans, Jazz, like I do and his voice and physical presence do something to me," Honey protested. "But that's not the problem."

"I'll say it's not! Y'all have got to see a shrink, Mother. Your personality is starting to fracture, I'm sure of it."

"I'll have a compatibility Astrological analysis done," her mood brightening as she thought of it. "That will get at the reasons for such a strong attraction."

"Use a shrink instead, Mother! Maybe a psychiatrist can

find out whatever bizarre reason you are attracted to a Funeral Director of all things. And one close to twenty-five years older than you."

"Didn't y'all hear about the late play write Arthur Miller and his latest and last love. She was a thirty-five-year-old artist and he was eighty-nine. That's what it's like with creative people, y'know. They talked for hours every day for months after they met. That's what happens when I'm with Tyler. I think I'm in love with the man."

"Y'all and that funeral director are not creative people. And how long did that Arthur Miller romance last?"

"It's lasted over two years until his death. Only one of my marriages ever lasted that long."

"Maybe you've developed a father complex?"

"My feelings toward Tyler are not daughterly, I can assure y'all." Honey went upstairs to contact her favourite Astrologist. Honey could feel her daughter's strong disapproval following her.

"Just because she's studying Psychology," Honey mused. "Personality fracture be damned. It's a Mars-Venus thing, I'm sure."

CHAPTER 8.
Virgie and Frank.

Virginia Kelly found herself dressing more carefully than usual as she prepared to go to the first rehearsal for next month's Church Christmas Concert. She knew that Frank Simpson would be there accompanying the choir and she wanted to look her best.

"I don't know about Gloria's wager," Virginia mused. Some part of her mind still told her the bet was connected to the Devil but another part of her mind reminded her that the church could make good use of sixty thousand dollars. It also told her that it would be better for Frank if she was the one that managed to interest him rather than worldly woman like Honey Pratt or Gloria Gustafson. Some part of her mind whispered that Honey in particular, coming from New Orleans, and maybe even Gloria, with her Hollywood morals, might be into Bondage practices or something even worse.

"Frank would be safer with me," she decided.

"I had better wear something other than black," she told herself. "It's about time I left the clothes behind that tell the world I was a wife of a minister."

Virgie found herself ploughing through all three closets in her bedroom in her search for something appealing. She found herself forming a huge pile of navy blue, brown and black clothes for the local consignment shop. Finally she located a pastel pink suit with a very feminine, white linen blouse and threw them on.

"Thank goodness," Virgie gave a sigh of relief as she added a black pearl necklace and earings that had been one of the few luxury items of jewelry that her austere, minister husband had allowed her in a rare moment of indulgence.

Virgie realised that her mind was extremely fuzzy. "Why am I so excited," she asked herself, at seeing Frank again, even if it is in the context of the upcoming Christmas concert. A strange mixture of thoughts was going through her mind. A sudden burst of insight told her that the excitement was from the thought of talking to an attractive, music-minded person of the opposite sex but Virgie immediately repressed such a thing.

"Of course it's the wager," she told herself, "the church could really use the money. But Frank is so good looking and we have music in common. Maybe he is ready now for a new love."

Virgie emitted a deep sigh as she headed for the door as reality set in.   "After all he is three years younger than I am. He's probably chasing women twenty years younger than I but I'll give it a try. The Church does need the organ."

Virgie's little Boston Bull Dog, Lazarus, barked with displeasure as his mistress reached the front door. Lazarus hated to be left behind.

"Tomorrow Laz. We'll walk in the morning." Virgie could hear Lazarus whine as she closed the door.

"Maybe tomorrow at the dog walking group I could manage to walk beside Frank and his Blue Healer, Mozart?" Virginia suddenly plotted. "I'll even ask him today if he wants to meet before the walk."

Frank Simpson was at the church early. He glanced around at the ladies already gathering for the choir practice as he sat down at the piano and set up his music on the stand.

Frank realised that he felt more alive now that the choir was meeting more often for the concert.

"I've been spending much too much time at home alone," he decided.

Frank knew that his wife's death from an undetected heart condition at sixty-five had caused him to go inward. But he was glad that he had spent the last eight years concentrating on nothing but his music. He had managed to compose many new classical and popular pieces that were being considered for publication by music publishers.

"Well, I do watch erotic videos quite often," Frank admitted to himself. "After all I made that vow when Angie died. That I'd never form another relationship with a woman again. That I'd never again risk the pain of losing someone I adored like I did Angie."

Frank rationalised that a man had to do something to satisfy his sexual urges.

"And besides, I find it extremely easy to compose original music scores after watching erotic videos."

"It's just that I'm sublimating my sexual urges," he rationalized, as at the same time he worried about the gradual increase in his erotic magazine subscriptions and video purchases over the years. Frank was a religious man and was not sure that God or his minister would approve of those activities.

"At least there's Mozart," Frank mused. "Thank heavens I bought the dog several days after Angie died. He's been such a great companion. If I didn't have him I probably wouldn't even get out for physical exercise at all."

Frank continued to wonder why he felt so much better. He had taken Mozart along the sea wall that morning with several of the men in the dog walking group and the blue in the ocean and sky seemed far more intense than he had ever known it. He even noticed for the first time the patterns that the sunlight and the clouds made on the mountains in the distance.

"It's like I've come through to the light at the end of the tunnel," the organist realised.

Frank's musing came to an end as he spotted Virgie Kelly entering the Church Hall. Frank did a double take.

"She's looking years younger; it must be that pastel pink suit."

Frank inhaled deeply in astonishment and took a closer look at one of his old friends. Virgie's husband and he had been dear friends. For the first time Frank realised that Virginia Kelly, his friend's widow, was a generously endowed, classic beauty.

"It's her cheekbones," he thought. "Classic and she looks years younger than her age." Frank noticed an unexpected warm feeling shoot through his heart as Virgie spotted him at the piano and moved in his direction.

"My God! Frank censured himself as he realised he was staring at Virginia's generous endowment. "She must be a forty, double D, at least."

"Good evening Frank," the organist's body reacted to the warmth in her voice as Virgie addressed him.

"You look lovely, Virginia," Frank could not believe himself. "That suit and blouse suit you to a 'T'." A part of Frank's mind urged him to ask Virgie out.

"Why thank you, you look very handsome yourself in that sports coat."

Virgie started as she noticed the leader of the choir coming into the room. He was signalling that the choir practice was about to begin.

"Would you and Mozart like to walk with Lazarus and me

tomorrow morning?" Virgie forced herself to ask, thinking of the need for the church to replace its organ.

Frank found himself arguing internally with the side of his mind urging him to hit on Virginia.

"What about my vow?" he argued with himself. "But she's so voluptuous. And she's a widow. Surely God wouldn't mind if I spent some time with her. After all she is a devout Christian." Frank impulsively made a decision he worried about later.

"Why, thank you Virginia, I usually walk with some of the men but let's meet early then at 7:15 a.m. at the start of the dog walk."

Virginia nodded discreetly as choir members formed around them and both her and Frank felt strange sensations going through their bodies as they arranged to meet.

"Gloria's right," Virginia mused. "I feel twenty years younger. The secret of youth must be sex or at least romance. I wonder where this is all going to lead." She tried to think of what she could possibly wear in the morning. "A n y t h i n g but black," she decided.

As he got home, Frank ignored his dog Mozart trying to engage him in playing tug and went through his collection of sports jackets looking for something that would appeal to Virginia.

"What about my vow?" Frank argued with himself. "Heavens, I'm only going to talk with the woman in a public place."

"That green sports jacket," he decided. "With a turtleneck, and I'll ask her out for lunch." Frank stared at his large collection of suits and ties with distaste.

"I really do need to go through these clothes," he acknowledged. "Too much black, navy blue and Grey. And all these suits and ties. They're not even worn much anymore."

Frank vowed to donate many of the expensive clothes to charity.

"I'll visit the new men's store at the mall," he decided. "That store has male fashions that are up to date." He stared at his collection of Playboy magazines and took a good look at what the men were wearing.

"I wonder if by some miracle Virgie would be up to watching some of these videos," he wondered as he stared at his large collection in his bookcase. "Can't take a chance on that, yet," he decided. "She is very religious after all. Might have to warm her up slowly. What am I thinking? I'm just going to talk to her and maybe have lunch."

Late the next afternoon Frank found himself ignoring the scratching of his dog, Mozart, and the whining the dog was making when his owner did not come immediately to let him in as he normally did. He was too busy passionately embracing Virginia on the comfortable chesterfield in his den. He had brought Virgie to his home in the pretext of rehearsing one of the numbers him and Virgie were doing for the Christmas concert. Things had gone so well he had wound up giving the lovely lady a kiss on her lips and one thing had led to another. Feeling her readiness, he had taken a chance and shown Virgie one of his erotic videos. Seeing the video had turned both of them on and Frank tried to calm himself as he realised Virgie was starting to undo his belt and zipper.

"What if you get really fond of her and she dies?" some part of his mind questioned. Virgie felt under his boxer shorts and Frank did not care what the answer to the question was. He pulled Virgie on top of him and started to undo her blouse.

"What about a condom?" Virgie somehow managed to worry about transmittable sexual diseases.

"There's no need," he groaned as she moved even closer

against him. He removed her bra and then her skirt. "I haven't had sex since Angie's death. What about you?"

Frank listened as Virgie told him that she had not had sex of any kind since her husband's death. He seized her tenderly and inserted himself into her.

"What am I doing?" some part of his mind briefly questioned his action but fell silent as Virgie provided him with some expert vaginal stimulation.

"My God," he thought, gasping with excitement. "This beats erotic videos all to Hell."

By the time Mozart was finally let in the front door Frank was eminently happy that he had made the decision to let a woman back into his life. Virgie was all but glowing and Frank realised that both of them had released an astounding amount of sexual repression in just one session of intense love making.

"Tomorrow," he asked her as he walked her to her car. "We'll walk the dogs together again at the dog park."

"I'm sure God wouldn't mind," Virgie assured him. He kissed her soundly again as she was getting into the car not even caring whether God minded or not.

CHAPTER 9.
Boxing Match.

Lorne Brooks found himself staring at Monica Mason's impressive physical attributes as she sat next to him in the smoke-filled boxing arena. Monica was wearing a tight fitting top and her expensive, satin pants revealed her well-muscled torso and upper body. Male boxing fans were staring at her in appreciation as she egged on the favourite at the championship boxing match they were watching.

"No wonder Malcolm dates her," Lorne thought as he experienced considerable jealousy at his uncle's successful promiscuity. "It's like this with everything. Malcolm is always the one to get the women, the money, the business deals, and the admiration of the Board of Directors rather than me, and before me, my father."

Lorne's jealousy of his uncle got even more pronounced when he thought of his own father's early retirement.

"He could never compete successfully with Malcolm either," Lorne realised. "That's why he retired early."

He mused about the injustice of his side of the family always being given the short end of the business the brothers inherited from his grandfather. His anger rose as he went over in his mind his father's early retirement and decline in mental functioning to the point he had to be placed into a nursing home.

"Alzheimer's, the doctors said. The doctors gave his father

only a few more years of deteriorated living. More anger struck as Lorne realised that his father's continuing deterioration was destroying his mother.

"Alzheimer's is a genetic condition," Lorne thought. "Good chance that Malcolm is developing it too. I just have to find some evidence for the Board of Directors."

"So Monica?" minutes later Lorne decided to probe Malcolm's latest love about his relative as Round three ended and the fighter's trainers attempted to revive the rapidly exhausting boxers. "What's it like dating my uncle? He's more than half a lifetime older than you."

Lorne's voice was loud as he was speaking above the boxing commentator's voice. The commentator suddenly stopped speaking just as Lorne asked his question and boxing fans around Lorne nudged each other, pointed at the sexy lady Lorne was talking to, and eagerly waited for her answer.

"Actually Malcolm's been very good to me," Lorne didn't like Monica's answer at all but the boxing fans within hearing range became even more curious. They craned their necks toward Lorne and Monica.

More jealousy rose to the surface in Lorne's mind as Monica elaborated on her answer.

"Malcolm's the person that got me into the Montgomery agency. I'll always be grateful for that."

"What about his performance in bed?" Lorne demanded loudly, desperate to find something indicating Malcolm was showing his age.

Several of the boxing fans moved closer and two got up and stood at the end of Lorne's row pretending they were discussing something.

"Surely a man that old can't satisfy you sexually?"

There was almost a movement of rows of people down toward Monica.

"Actually, Malcolm's very good at it, " Monica testified to Lorne's increased discomfort and the delight of the boxing fans within hearing distance. "He's very experienced, you know. Know's all the moves. He's taught me a lot." Lorne choked and the boxing fans sighed. Round four started before Lorne could get Monica to be a little more explicit. Lorne was forced to wait for the end of the round before proceeding.

"Can the old boy hang on until you get satisfied?" he blurted a little too loudly at the same moment the announcer ceased his talking again. The people around Lorne waited anxiously for the answer. Monica hesitated. She seemed to be weighing the question carefully.

"Actually he holds up rather well. Older men do, you know, require more time to reach a climax. It works out quite well."

"What about frequency?" Lorne was getting more and more desperate.

People around him held their conversations back and anxiously awaited Monica's answer.

"He does use Viagra," Monica informed him. "He's always ready when I am. Frequency is not a problem."

"How do you know that?"

"I've seen him take a small blue pill before he takes me to bed. Figure that's what he's using."

"At last," Lorne thought, oblivious to the nudges and stares of people all around him. Some of the elderly, male, boxing fans were now considering using Viagra themselves and their wives were wishing they would. "Something about Malcolm's health that could be used against him. Viagra. Perhaps Malcolm's blood flow was not as strong as it should be."

"Could be affecting his brain cells? I'll try and bribe someone in his Doctor's office," Lorne plotted. "Maybe I can obtain his medical records."

"Why are you asking me all these questions about Malcolm?" Monica demanded as Round five started.

"Just wondering why you were so attracted to him," Lorne answered, anxious not to blow his cover.

Lorne sighed as Round five gave him time to improvise questions about Monica rather than Malcolm to throw her off. Lorne felt jealousy rising strongly again as he went over both Linda's and Monica's answers to his questions. He realised that both women, even though they were quite different from each other, had one thing in common.

"They're both loyal to my uncle," he cursed under his breath. "Surely the man isn't worth their loyalty."

As Lorne stopped his luxury sedan in front of Monica's house he reached over to kiss her but Monica would have none of it.

"Malcolm wouldn't stand for that," she told him in no uncertain terms. "We have an agreement. I can date others but not have sex with them."

Monica's rejection resulted in Lorne becoming furious. Rage at Malcolm surged in Lorne's mind.

"Am I too young for you?" he asked sarcastically.

"Actually a little too old," she answered. "But thanks for taking me to the championship match. Enjoyed it a lot!"

Monica closed the car door and moved toward her residence. Lorne drove off in a fury with his car's tires smoking.

CHAPTER 10.
Esther and Art.

Gus Gustafson kept a close watch on the dogs frolicking in the mouth of the river at the Dog Walking Park. He had brought Inuvik and Gigi to the park for exercise. Malcolm Brooks was still in the hospital. Surgery had been performed on his broken leg. Gus missed him. Art Maloney was standing with him watching his Greyhound, Bookkeeper, swim about with Inuvik and Gigi.

Loud barking alerted Gus and Art to the fact that they were no longer alone. Pegasus, Esther Goodenough's Wheaton Terrier, and Cleo, Linda Daniel's Doberman, joined Gus and Art as their mistresses reached him. Gus marvelled that Esther, an eighty-year-old lady, had managed to raise the big Wheaton Terrier.

Gus yelled as Inuvik lunged to chase one of the Blue Herons that frequented the river mouth. Inuvik immediately stopped his pursuit and joined the other dogs. Gus turned his attention to Esther. He realised that she was having great difficulty holding on to her Wheaton Terrier long enough to free him from his leash. Linda Daniels had let go of Cleo and the large Doberman was heading out into the water. Pegasus was lunging, trying to join her.

Suddenly Pegasus pulled forward and to Gus's horror the older woman lost her footing and crashed onto the rocky, barnacled strewn sand. She finally let go of the leash as Pegasus plunged into the water pulling Esther with him. Art Maloney flew to the woman's rescue.

Gus and Linda reached Art and Esther at the same time and were relieved to hear their dog walking friend laughing ruefully. Art helped her to her feet and noticed she was having great trouble with her right knee.

"Oh no, it's snapped out again," Esther laughed. "Third time this month I've done a pratfall in front of witnesses."

"Are you all right?" Linda questioned the older lady as Art supported her weight.

"I'll be all right," Esther reassured her. "The knee takes a while to snap back. But my clothes will dry."

"You need one of those electric leashes," Art told Esther.

"I need more than that, " Esther laughed.

Esther took a step but her right knee wasn't up to it. Art prevented another fall by grabbing her firmly around the waist and holding her up.

"However did you raise that big dog of yours?"

"It wasn't easy. That's why my right knee is damaged. My large dog is forever putting pressure on it when he pulls and particularly when he lunges."

"Remember Turk saying radio collar leashes were for sale somewhere Gus?"

Gus Gustafson reached for his wallet and pulled out a card.

"The Giant Dog pets store in the Metropolitan Mall."

"All right Esther my dear, we are going to go and pick up one of those leashes for Pegasus. Right now!"

Linda and Gus watched in amazement at Art, who was himself eighty-five years old, half carry Esther toward the parking lot. Fortunately Pegasus spotted her leaving and moved away from Cleo to swim in to shore. Art whistled for his Greyhound, Bookkeeper, and the dog dutifully headed to shore as well.

Gus and Linda stared at Art and Esther disappearing down the walkway with Pegasus and Bookkeeper galloping joyfully in front of them. Art had his arm firmly around Esther's waist to support her.

"Gloria's at it again, isn't she?" he confronted a startled Linda Daniels.

"At it again?" Linda bluffed. She felt her face redden with embarrassment.

"All these couples. Tyler and Honey, Art and Esther, and I nearly fell over in shock when I spotted Frank Simpson having lunch with Virgie Kelly in my favourite restaurant the other day. I swear they were playing sex games under the table."

Linda tried to avoid Gus's direct question by suggesting that it must be the Mistletoe everywhere for the coming Christmas Season.

"Who's she got you linked up with?" Gus queried with disbelief in his voice. "Malcolm Brooks, I bet."

Linda swallowed hard. She did not want to admit that she had been spending day after day with Malcolm at the hospital. Particularly after his leg had to be operated on.

"Oh, we're just friends," Linda sputtered. She didn't want to share her private longings for Malcolm with anyone, particularly Gus.

"Sure," Gus said, "friends like Tyler and Honey, I suppose."

Angie looked in the direction Gus was pointing. Honey Pratt and Tyler Thompson were kissing passionately down by the park entrance.

"Oh, I think he took her to a Dixieland Jazz Festival. They must have hit it off. I guess it all does seem rather suspicious."

"What's the wager this time?" Gus demanded.

Linda could feel the heat creeping into her face. She imagined it must be bright red with embarrassment. She could not bring herself to tell Gloria's husband the terms of his wife's wager.

"Let me guess?" Linda's face turned even redder as Gus continued to interrogate her.

"A large sum to the person or persons who get a new boyfriend by Christmas?" Gus queried.

"How did you know?"

"Gloria's incorrigible. Every time the dog club members start grouping according to their sex, Gloria starts up one of these wagers."

"Is it true that you and she have an open marriage?" Linda asked.

"Oh, she told you that too, did she? And what else is different about the bet this time?"

"You're included in it."

Gus snorted. "My God, Linda are you interested?"

Linda choked. "Uh, actually I'm rather tied up with Malcolm right now, just as a friend, but you know who is interested in you."

"I can't wait."

"Esther."

Gus looked astonished.

"Esther is interested in me!"

Linda told Gus that Esther had insisted on his name being included in the eligible men for the wager.

"Right."

Linda relaxed slightly as Gus scanned the horizon looking after Esther and Art Maloney disappearing in the distance.

"Missed my chance did I?" Gus laughed.

Fifteen minutes later Art pulled into a parking stall at the Metropolitan Mall. Esther was still brushing the sand and barnacles off her clothes.

"The pet store is inside."

Art got out and opened the door for Esther.

"How about lunch first?"

"Why not?" Art was surprised at Esther's invitation. "The dogs will be all right. They're in the shade."

"You can bring some water back for them from the restaurant."

Esther limped noticeably as she headed in the direction of the restaurant. Art immediately put his arm around her waist to steady her. Esther smiled as she realised she had gotten the attention of one of the eligible men. She leaned against Art and thanked him warmly. Art noticed that he felt glad to be having lunch with another human being.

"I'm spending far too much time on the stock trends on the Internet," he confessed to Esther. "I'm afraid I'm becoming rather obsessive about predicting the stocks that are going to rise."

"You really should make an effort to get out more," Esther said to him as they rounded the corner.

"Perhaps you'll let me show me how the electric leash works?"

"I'd be delighted, Arthur, my dear. How about tomorrow morning at the dog park?"

The next morning Esther spotted Art waiting for her in the parking lot of the dog walking park. She noted with approval that Art was dressed in a sporty track suit that had him looking years younger. He was standing with his Greyhound, Bookkeeper on a leash and holding the electric leash they had purchased in his free hand. Esther released

Pegasus who careened over to Bookkeeper and she limped over to Art.

"How's the knee?" he asked.

"A little better. You look very sporty in that track suit."

Esther noted Art's smile broaden considerably at her praise.

"Lunch after our session?"

"Thank you, Arthur Dear, I'll look forward to it."

Esther smiled herself as Art queried whether she was free or lunch or dinner every day that week. She quickly agreed and he beamed some more as he attached the radio collar and electric leash to Pegasus and beeped a warning for Pegasus to stop pulling. Pegasus lunged after Bookkeeper again and Art pressed the buzzer that sent a mild electric shock through the radio collar of the attached leash. Pegasus stopped suddenly and moved toward Art. The large dog gave him a puzzled look.

"No pull!" Art directed. He moved forward again in the direction of Bookkeeper who was heading for the ocean access. Pegasus watched Bookkeeper disappearing and whined but he did not tug on the leash.

"He's getting the message unusually fast. Smart dog."

Twenty minutes and two shocks later Art handed the leash to Esther.

"You try it."

The dog started to pull toward Bookkeeper who was barking at him from the ocean. Esther pushed the warning button. It beeped and the large Wheaton Terrier stopped in his tracks.

"He's got it," Art Maloney shouted. "Start walking toward the parking lot."

Esther obeyed Art and was amazed to find her dog moving

with her. He matched his gait to hers and although whining to go back toward Bookkeeper, did not lunge.

"Success!" Art Maloney rushed up to Pegasus. He removed the electric collar from his neck and the large dog looked at him as if asking if he could go after Bookkeeper.

"Go join him," Art motioned toward the water and the dog bounced away. Within a minute he was frolicking with Bookkeeper. Esther put her arms around Art and thanked him.

"We'll give them twenty minutes and then we'll go for lunch."

CHAPTER 11.
Down Memory Lane Care Home.

Bea Broughton came back to consciousness again with a shock. As the drowsiness caused by whatever drug they were giving her wore off again her eyes started to focus and she stared at the white walls and white furniture in the room she was in with disbelief. Horror filled her mind as she recognised she was back in the Agitation Room of the Down Memory Lane Care Home Alzheimer's Wing. Bea flashbacked to her original tour of the Extended Care Facility her son had brought her to and experienced again the horror and betrayal she felt when she found out her son and daughter-in-law were taking advantage of her signed Power of Attorney to place her in the home against her wishes.

"They keep drugging me," the petite woman realized. "I wonder how long I've been here now." She realised she was still wearing her watch. She stared at the digital date. Panic struck and nausea gnawed at her stomach.

"It's over three weeks now!"

Intense negative emotions overcame her as she relived again her shock and horror at what happened at the end of the guided tour of the home. John and Orphelia had disappeared and she had been taken to the Director's office and told that her son and daughter-in-law were placing her here for her own good.

Beatrice shook at her memory of the event and of her

shouting in defiance that there was no way she was remaining in the home. She remembered the Director coldly showing her a copy of her Power of Attorney and telling her to appreciate her son's thoughtful actions. Bea remembered loudly demanding to phone her lawyer and the Director pushing a button on his desk. Her mind chilled as she remembered two staff members seizing her, a syringe being pushed into her arm and losing consciousness shortly afterwards.

"I've got to get out of here somehow!" Bea felt herself going into a frenzy again. "Every time they catch me trying to escape they drug me."

Bea went over her attempts to get out of the building. At first they had left her cane but took it away when they spotted her out in the parking lot. She had been heading for the woods behind the lot not far away in the distance. The second time she had used the wheel chair they had left her in at the hair dressing room. She had made it down the elevator when the hair stylist had vacated the room but the receptionist had intercepted her as she tried to leave through a side door. The third time she had pulled herself into a laundry chute when she had been left in the bath tub alone. Despite her situation Bea broke into a hearty laugh as she remembered the expression on the fellow removing laundry from the chute when she landed in the care home laundry one floor below. He had pressed the care home alarm and the myriads of staff members who had come running had witnessed her stark, naked self being forcibly removed from the laundry room.

Bea's heart palpitated rapidly as she went over her daughter-in-law's last visit. She had not even seen her son or her grandchildren since he had placed her in the home. Orphelia had told her that John could not bring himself to visit unless she could tell him that his mother had finally seen the light and agreed to remain in the care home. Orphelia also told her that she would even bring her grandchildren to visit provided Bea would at least pretend to be happy with the place.

Bea realised that she was being blackmailed and that her future appeared to be in Orphelia's hands. She shuddered at the thought and she forced herself to take a deep breath to try and stop her heart palpitations. Adrenaline shot into her bloodstream. It gave her the courage to raise herself in the bed.

"I'm not wearing a restraint vest this time," Bea realised. She looked around the room but there was no sign of her cane.

"They realise I can't go far without that cane," Bea noted with more panic filling her mind. "They've removed it again." Then hope lit up her heart as she spotted her purse. It was on one of the end tables.

"They've finally returned it."

Bea slithered out of the bed, clutched onto the furniture and agonizingly made her way over to the end table. She collapsed into a chair and looked into the purse hoping to find something that would help her get out of the place. Turk O'Brien's card he had left her fell out. His phone number was on the card. Bea frantically ran her eyes over the room looking for a phone. She sighed as she spotted a phone on another end table. Bea stood up holding the card but her leg gave way. She fell to the floor. Bea used her arms and one good leg to slowly crawl over to the end table. She reached up and managed to grab the phone. It came crashing down to the floor.

Bea picked up the receiver, heard a dial tone and dialled the number nine hoping to get an outside line. Another dial tone came on. Bea dialled Turk's number. Her hopes sank as the phone kept ringing. Finally a voice mail instructed her to leave a message.

"Turk, it's Bea Broughton. I need your help. My son has placed me in the Down Memory Lane Care Home against my will. Please get me out of here." Bea found herself breaking down into uncontrollable sobs. She managed to replace the phone on the end table and tried to pull herself together. After several minutes she managed to drag herself over to the end table where her purse was and placed Turk's card back into her purse.

"They'll search that," she anticipated. "If they realise I've made a phone call. I've got to remember the number."

Bea repeated the phone number to herself continuously as she dragged herself over to the bed. She managed to pull herself back into the bed with the help of the bed clothes. Just as she made it back into the bed the door came crashing open. Bea kept her eyes closed hoping they would think she was still sleeping.

"You must have been mistaken," Bea recognized the Director's cold voice.

"I'm sure her phone light on the switchboard was lit up."

"Give her another shot. And remove that purse. We don't want her contacting anyone."

Bea forced herself to remain motionless as a hand seized her arm, a prick reached her consciousness and deep sleep overtook her again.

At the Tyneburst Cafe Turk O'Brien had a strange feeling that something was very wrong. Dogzilla seemed to sense a problem, too, and the large Rottweiler broke into a whine. Trump licked his face in sympathy. Turk reached for his cell phone and called his own phone at home. He coded in his remote access for his voice mail and chills ran up and down his spine as he listened to Bea's frantic message. Turk lost his appetite as the seriousness of Bea's plight reached him when he listened to her sobbing. As the voice mail ceased Turk O'Brien jumped to his feet, left enough money to cover his uneaten dinner, freed Dogzilla and Trump from around the base of the table and ran toward his car.

"Something's come up," he shouted at the amazed hostess as he fled the restaurant. Once in his car Turk phoned the Directory Service and asked for the phone number of the Down Memory Lane Care Home. He punched the numbers in with his big fingers. A woman's voice answered.

"Do you have a tour of your facilities?" he asked. "I'm looking for a place for my widowed father?"

Turk left a fictitious name as the female voice gave him an appointment for the next afternoon. Turk asked for directions to the facility and his heartbeat slowed somewhat as he realised that at least he finally knew what had happened to Bea and where she had disappeared to.

"It's my fault," Turk blamed himself. He felt mortified. "I should have tried to find out what had happened instead of believing she had rejected me." Turk turned on his ignition and moved off in the direction of Bea's house. He made it in record time but was horrified as he drove into Bea's driveway. A large "For Sale" sign was on the front lawn. As Turk opened his door and got out a dog's howling came from behind Bea's fence. Turk realised that Bea's Pomeranian, Angus, was out in the backyard. There were no lights on in the house or any sign of movement. The front driveway was empty..

Turk freed Dogzilla from the back seat but kept Trump in.

Angus wailed again, a long, eery wail.

"Fetch Angus," Turk commanded. He pointed in the direction of the wailing. The large Rottweiler approached Bea's fence and looked back at his master as he reached the edge. Angus barked frantically.

"Fetch Angus" Turk commanded again. Dogzilla went back toward Turk, turned and made a rush at the fence. He cleared it with a single bound. There was a yelp from Angus from behind the fence. Turk's heart warmed as seconds later his dog reappeared with a silent Angus held firmly in his mouth. The little dog seemed to know that Dogzilla was trying to help him and was staying absolutely still. Turk took the little fellow in his arms and stroked him. The dog whined pitifully. Turk realised he could feel Angus's ribs.

"He's not been eating."

"Good Boy!" Turk praised Dogzilla. He looked around to see if any of the neighbours appeared to be watching. No one seemed to be in sight. Turk placed the dogs in with Trump in the back seat. Angus whined pitifully and Trump licked his face. Turk pulled out of the driveway rather sedately for him.

"Don't worry, Bea. I've got Angus and I'll get you soon," he vowed to the absent women.

CHAPTER 12.
Escalation.

Frank Simpson noticed that Virginia Kelly was having great difficulty restraining her emotions as he and the woman he had let into his life gradually moved into more and more advanced sex techniques. They had started to try out some of the things they were watching on his erotic videos. But as they got more and more adventurous Virgie began to express growing doubts about their intimate activities. Frank had managed to get her to watch one of his videos that had a respected clergyman telling his audience that sex practices past the missionary position were permissible provided that the couple were married. Then he had impulsively proposed to Virginia. To his surprise, after a few intimate kisses, she had agreed.

"We'll have to keep this a secret for a while," Frank nodded as Virginia told him about the need to introduce the matter gradually to her son and daughter.

"My children aren't going to be too thrilled, either," Frank acknowledged.

"We'll have to have a pre-nuptial agreement drawn up. That should make them more receptive to the idea if their inheritance is not threatened."

Frank agreed and told Virginia he would have his lawyer draft such an agreement for both of them.

"We'll marry in the Spring," Virginia promised. "That

way we have time to gradually let the kids know something's going on."

"Read this," Frank remembered demanding, after he had handed Virgie a copy of 'The Joy of Sex.'

"For the future, of course."

The next time they met for lunch it was Virgie that started the sex games under the table in the restaurant. By the time Frank drove Virgie home he was fully sexually aroused.

"We're getting married anyway," Virgie blurted as they sat beside the sex toys they had purchased at an erotic video store. "God shouldn't mind."

"God won't mind!" Frank told her with considerable certainty in his voice.   "Let's try my house this time."

As the Boston Bull Dog, Lazarus, greeted them warmly at the door, Virgie gave him a slight pat and a large dog biscuit. She closed the front door, pulled Frank against her and dragged him into her bedroom.

An overjoyed Frank used several of the new tools to heighten both him and Virgie's enjoyment of the sex act. She responded passionately.

"We should buy some more videos," Virgie stated at the end of their session. "The ones that have bondage procedures in them.

"Indeed!" Frank agreed.

"After all we do want to be prepared for marriage."

"Absolutely," Frank agreed. "Pick you up at six o'clock."

CHAPTER 13.
Casing the Care Home.

Linda had been visiting Malcolm every day at the hospital despite her vacillating feelings about him. She was still finding the man attractive despite the large gap in their ages and the existence of a much younger girlfriend. The door of his room was closed when she got there. She knocked timidly on it.

"Come in," Malcolm's voice instructed her as he opened the door himself. He was wearing a robe and he was using crutches.

"You're walking," Linda's voice betrayed her happiness at Malcolm's quick recuperation.

"Right," he replied. "I think I'm going to be sent home sometime this week."

"Give the Dog Park a break for a while! Let me know when you're going to be released and I'll get Trump back from Turk O'Brien for you."

"I'm eager to get back to the office. Heaven knows what that nephew of mine has done in my absence."

Malcolm's words reminded Linda of her unsettling lunch and date with Lorne Brooks. She decided to take a chance on confiding her suspicions about his nephew.

"Malcolm, forgive me for interfering in your business life, but I think that nephew of yours has his eye on your position."

"That will be the day," Malcolm replied. "That man is a horse's ass. If he wasn't my brother's son I would never have moved him up as high as I have."

"He was asking me if I noticed any deterioration in your memory, judgement or cognitive awareness?"

"The bastard!"

Linda realised that Malcolm was becoming very upset.

"I'm sorry, I shouldn't have mentioned it but if I were you I'd have a battery of psychological tests done. Just to prove your mind is in as good a state as your body."

Malcolm looked at her in surprise. He seemed to calm down.

"That's a very good suggestion, my dear!"

Linda gave him a warm pat on his hand.

Malcolm sat down on the bed and started to return her grasp with his own but stopped as Turk O'Brien suddenly charged into the room

"Good you're here too," he said to a startled Linda. "I'm going to need both of you."

"Whatever for?"

"It's Bea Broughton," Linda felt the desperation and concern in the Paul Newman lookalike's voice, "she's locked up in an Extended Care Home against her wishes.

"Good Lord," Linda immediately emphasized with the plight of her acquaintance in the Dog Walking Club.

"By whom?"

"Apparently her son John and his wife. There's a 'For Sale' sign on her house."

"How do you know where she is? We've all been wondering where Bea has been for weeks."

"I got a call on my cell phone. Last night. Bea left a message on my voice mail telling me where she was and asked me to get her out."

"You'll need a lawyer," Malcolm advised.

"Won't do no good," Turk assured him. "Son's got a signed Power of Attorney. Told her to revoke it but I guess there wasn't time."

"What about Angus, her dog?" Linda worried about the canine. She knew how attached Bea was to him.

"He's with Dogzilla and Trump," Turk explained. "Poor dog. I'm just managing to get him to eat something. Have to hand feed him."

"How did he get there?"

"Kidnapped him." Turk stated.

Malcolm listened with growing alarm as Turk told him and Linda that he needed to kidnap Bea, too, out of the Care Home. That he had an appointment for a tour of the place that afternoon and that he would make sure he located what Bea had called the "Agitation Room" and get her out of there.

"That's against the law, Turk," Malcolm tried to reason with the distraught man. "You've got to do something through legal channels."

"She could be dead by then," Turk argued. "You don't know how some of these facilities handle patients."

"Turk, kidnapping in this state is a felony. Particularly if you try and take her across the state line. You could spend the rest of your life in prison."

"No matter!" Turk shot back. Malcolm and Linda realised that the big man was beyond reason.

"How can we help?"

"Need you and Malcolm to come with me. Have to have help casing this place."

"I'll come with you, Turk," Linda made up her mind. "Malcolm's just managed to get up on crutches."

Malcolm felt horrified. He suddenly realised that he did not want anything happening to Linda.

"I'll do it," he said in a tone that inferred that both Turk and Linda were out of their minds. "I'm the one that owes Turk, Linda. Remember?"

"Good. Keep that hospital garb on," Turk instructed. "Maybe we can pass you off as my elderly, demented father."

"My God!" Malcolm felt like he was losing his mind but he obediently lifted himself off the bed and placed the crutches under his arms.

"We'll have to go down the back staircase, the hospital won't release me yet, I know."

"Your health insurance won't cover you if you do that," Linda warned. "And what about your nephew if anything goes wrong."

"To Hell with his health insurance," Turk motioned both of them to follow him out the door.

"You stay here," Malcolm told Linda. "I'll deal with Lorne if the situation necessitates it. I'm coming with you Turk."

All three of them started for the door. Linda watched apprehensively as Turk grabbed one of the wheelchairs from the hallway and motioned for Malcolm to sit in it. When they reached the side staircase without interference Turk picked Malcolm and the wheelchair up in his strong arms and carried both of them down the stairs despite Malcolm's protests.

"Taking him for lunch," Turk informed the nurse who stared at them in disbelief near the bottom of the stairs.

"The cafeteria is at the rear."

Turk pointed Malcolm's wheelchair in the direction of the cafeteria but once he was out of sight of the nurse he moved through a side door.

At the parking lot Linda got into the back seat of Turk's

car with Dogzilla, Trump and Angus. The little Pomeranian greeted her like an old friend. Trump barked joyously at Malcolm and attempted to jump into the front seat as Malcolm sat down in the passenger side but Turk's rough command to "freeze" had the large sheep dog drop motionless onto the back seat.

"What did you do to him?" Malcolm demanded.

"Taught him some manners."

Malcolm looked at his dog. The big Sheep Dog stared back at him with pleading in his eyes. Malcolm reached into the back seat to pat Trump but the dog leaped up again and attempted to climb into the front seat.

Turk issued a curse and ordered Trump to freeze . Again the dog slumped onto the seat and sat immobile.

"You should rent yourself out as a dog trainer," Linda commented.

"Radio collar, works real well."

"I was going to get one of those. Thanks, Turk."

"What are we going to do when we get to the Care Home?"

Turk told them the plan he had quickly put together when he discovered Linda in the room as well as Malcolm. He told them that Malcolm would have to pretend that he was his father, that he was in the final stages of Alzheimers, and needed an immediate placement in the care facility. He said that way they could tour the place and might find out where Bea was located.

"What about me?" Linda queried.

"You're my sister."

Malcolm and Linda exchanged glances.

"I'm not old enough to be your father."

Turk handed him his cap with 'Molson Indie' blazoned in red on the front.

"Put this on. They'll think your hair is completely grey like it is on your sides. Make sure your voice sounds ancient."

Malcolm realised his hair dye was receding.

"Linda doesn't look anything like you."

Turk handed her his sunglasses.

"Wear these."

Linda started as she looked at the glasses. They had a naked lady ingrained on the side pieces. She swallowed and put them on anyway.

"They're too big!"

Turk reached for them and twisted the ear holds to make them smaller. Linda tried them on again. They stayed in place.

At the care home Turk found a parking space in the shade for the dogs. As he and Linda wheeled Malcolm into the lobby, Turk gave the fake name he had used for the appointment to the receptionist. Within minutes a tall man in a business suit introduced himself to Turk.

"Mr. Thomas, welcome, I'm Dr. Jim, the Director of this Facility. I'll show you personally around."

Turk stared at the man and managed to force himself to shake his proffered hand. He fought off his urge to grab him by the throat and demand to know where Bea was.

"This is my father, Louis, and my sister Linda."

The Director turned to Malcolm and put out his hand.

"Welcome Mr. Thomas."

"This ain't the chicken place," Malcolm ignored the offered handshake and did an excellent imitation of an angry Alzheimer victim well into deterioration. His voice even sounded really old. Linda stared at him in appreciation.

"I'm afraid my father's perception is distorted," she explained. "We had to tell him we were taking him out for chicken to get him into the car."

"Not to worry, we're used to our patients getting agitated. We even have a special room to calm them down."

"Where is it?" Turk demanded. He realized the Director was referring to the "Agitation Room" that Bea had mentioned.

"Oh, we'll get to it during the tour. First I want to show you our Down Memory Lane activity rooms. We've got both a 'Marriage Memory Room' for the ladies and a 'Your Woodwork Memory Room' for the men."

Turk and Linda looked at each other and followed the Director down the hall as he pushed Malcolm forward. It was obvious that the Director did not suspect a thing. They passed through several corridors with private rooms on each side and came to a room with a woodworking sign on its door. The Director pushed Malcolm through as Linda opened the door for him. Inside the room everyone stared at the array of woodworking tools on the table and shelves lining the room.

Turk O'Brien picked up one of the saws and a piece of wood. He tried the saw out on the wood but it did not cut very well.

"Oh, these aren't real tools, Mr. O'Brien, just replicas. We just want to stir our Alzheimer's patients memories not have them do any real woodwork."

"This ain't the chicken place!" Malcolm complained again.

The Director quickly wheeled Malcolm out the door and down the hall. They came to a stop at a door labelled "Marriage Memories." Linda followed the Director into an all white room. It was filled with wedding memorabilia. A life-size mannequin of a bride and groom were in one corner. Another corner held a table gaily decorated for a wedding complete with a hanging banner, balloons and tiny treat baskets for the guests. Other wedding items were display along the shelves and on the furniture in the room.

"You would be amazed how this room stimulates the memories of our ladies."

Malcolm and Linda looked at each other with raised eyebrows.

"This ain't the chicken place. I ain't getting married again. You're not leaving me here in Las Vegas!" Malcolm shouted in his deranged, elderly voice.

"I'm afraid my father is quite demented," Linda apologised.

"No problem. I'll show you the 'Agitation Room.' That's where we handle patients like your father when they become difficult."

The Director wheeled Malcolm out through the door and over to an elevator. Linda and Turk followed them onto the elevator as the door opened. The Director stepped out into a basement area. Down the hall one of the rooms was labelled "Agitation Room."

The room was blinding in its whiteness. The walls, the bedding, the furniture and the decorations were all white. Even the paintings on the wall were black and white drawings. Turk spotted the white phone on one of the white end tables. A slow fury was growing in his brain.

"That must have been the phone Bea used," he thought.

"Get me out of this place!" Malcolm yelled. "There's too much white. Are we in Heaven? Where is St. Peter?"

Soothing music was playing in the background and white fish were circling around a white-edged, goldfish bowl.

"An agitated patient stays here until they calm down," the Director explained.

"Could we see what the patients' rooms look like?" Turk demanded.

"Next on our tour."

He wheeled Malcolm out the door. They went back up the elevator and got off on the second floor. Turk noted that the facility had six floors.

"We assign patients according to the amount of deterioration they are exhibiting. Floor six has the most deteriorated men and women. Floor one holds the patients with the least problems."

"And the other floors?" Linda inquired.

"In-between and new arrivals," the Director explained. "Until they adjust and we get a good idea about their strengths and weaknesses."

Turk realized he had just been told where Bea was being kept. He tried to think of a plausible excuse to visit Floors two to five.

The Director pushed Malcolm through one of the doors on Floor two and Turk and Linda followed. No one was in the room and Turk had a good look around. A comfortable bed was provided as well as a dresser. Turk had a good look out the window. He noted that the dormitories were not far from the parking lot.

"You're welcome to bring a few pieces of your father's favourite furniture," the Director's voice signalled the end of the tour.

"You're not leaving me in Heaven!" Malcolm yelled.

"We'll get you some chicken, Father," Linda assured him in a soothing voice.

"Thanks so much," Linda shook the Director's hand. "We'll be back sometime next week to make the arrangements. How soon could my father enter?"

"Within the month after you've signed the papers and we get a copy of your father's medical records." The Director sighed as the sound of hammering reached through the walls of his office.

"As you can hear, we're just in the midst of adding an addition onto the upper floors. It should be finished anytime. I've got the construction crew working through the night along with the laundry and night staff to get the addition completed as fast as possible. We will have room for your father within a month."

Turks' ears perked up. He listened to the construction sounds. He had noticed laundry workers moving about the ward picking up towels and bedding.

"I'll come back later tonight," he plotted. "Dressed in laundry worker clothes."

"We'll be in touch," Turk told the director as he wheeled Malcolm out of the room. Linda followed and Turk moved Malcolm and the wheelchair back to his car. The dogs were staring out the window and wagged their tails as the trio reappeared.

"What now?" Malcolm asked as Turk helped him into the front seat.

"I'll come back tonight dressed in laundry worker clothes." The construction crew workers work through the night. Everyone must be a little distracted by the noise and confusion."

"You'll need help," Linda stated. "I'll come and contact some of the others. Bea has many friends in the Dog Walking Club."

"I'll do it," Malcolm protested. "I'm the one that owes Turk."

"We won't be able to spring you from the hospital later."

"So don't take me back."

Malcolm Brooks put up quite an argument to be the

person to return with Turk. He did not want Linda to be the one implicated in the kidnapping if something went wrong but Turk overruled him. He told Malcolm that someone on crutches or in a wheelchair would not fit into the disguises they were going to use.

"Linda, I'll pick you and the others up at seven o'clock tonight," Turk ordered.

"Right. I'll buy some ER outfits. They're popular with everyone now. The laundry people wear them."

"Imagine them stacking the patients by how deteriorated they are with the worst on the highest floor and the best ones on the first."

Linda stared at the wealthy industrialist. She had never detected compassion coming from him before.

"You're right Malcolm. That's incredible."

"Likely stacked with the most spirited at the top and the most placid at the bottom. Harder to escape from the top floors, I imagine."

"And what about those memory rooms. Do you think they would be effective with Alzheimer's patients?"

"There's no study to support that. Looks like they are just trying to convince the families of their prospective clients that they are the cutting edges."

"Snake Oil Salesman," Turk sneered. "After money and lots of it if you ask me."

"And that 'Agitation Room.' Used to drug anyone putting up resistance, I imagine."

CHAPTER 14.
Rescue Attempt.

Virginia Kelly ignored the insistent phone ringing as she passionately made love to Frank Simpson on her four poster beds. He was attached firmly in a bondage position on the old-fashioned bed and she was on top of him dressed in a dominatrix costume cracking a rawhide whip.

"I don't know what's coming over Virgie," Frank sighed to himself. "All these sex toys, erotic videos, the costumes and the bondage equipment. What have I created?"

Frank marvelled at Verges rapid advancement to them once he had taken a risk and shown her some of his videos. After several erotic movies, which Virgie seemed to appreciate once she got over her shock, he had initiated more erotic sexual foreplay with her during their increasingly more frequent sex sessions. Virginia had been a quick learner and borrowed some of his erotic literature to find out more about foreplay. Next he had introduced a vibrator into their session and lent her his copy of "Beyond the Missionary Position." Soon they were visiting sex toy stores and trying out things the clerks recommended. He realised that Virgie and he were highly attracted to one another but he was beginning to wonder about some of their practices, given their advanced ages.

Frank marvelled that it had been Virgie who had suggested they try some of the bondage positions they had been watching in the erotic videos.

"Don't worry it's just repressed sexuality," some voice in his head shouted at him. "Enjoy it while you can."

"Virgie, Frank Simpson yelled. "You better answer the phone. It might be your son or daughter coming over or something."

Virgie ignored Frank's shouting. She was used to him getting rather vocal during their sessions.

"Virgie, the phone!" he shouted as loud as he could. His words finally penetrated her brain. She dropped the whip and reached over for the phone.

"Hello," she managed as she disengaged herself from Frank. Virgie did her best to separate the sexual fantasy she was in the midst of experiencing with Frank from the strange message she was getting from Linda Daniels on the phone.

"Bea Broughton needs help," she explained to Frank as the delightful sensuality she had discovered with him finally gave way to the reality Linda was trying to tell her.

"Bea needs rescuing, " she explained to Frank. "Her son's placed her into a care home against her will and keeping her drugged. We've got to go to a meeting."

"Virgie, you better release me from these handcuffs if that's the case."

Virgie shook her head to clear it, stood up and started to search for the key to the handcuffs. She always had trouble locating it and Frank got a little irritated at the length of time she took to locate it.

"It's on the bookcase, Virgie, I watched you this time."

Virgie picked up the key and freed Frank. He helped her remove her dominatrix costume and they placed all their accessories in the large trunk that Virgie had purchased for their lovemaking.

"We'll finish this later," Frank promised.

"I promised Linda we would meet her in two hours," Virgie explained. Both Frank and Virgie changed back into their usual clothes and little Lazarus, Virgie's dog, was very happy to have his black cat outfit removed.

Back at the hospital Linda was using her cell phone to contact other members of the Dog Walking Club. Linda helped Malcolm off with his robe and he worked his way back into his bed again and listened to the conversations. He was amazed at the number of people wanting to help. By the time Linda had finished phoning he realised that all of the regular dog walking members were willing to put themselves at risk to help get Bea out of her precarious situation.

"Even Art Maloney and Frank Simpson are coming," Linda informed him. "Imagine, persons of their status. What if someone recognizes them?"

"Let them drive the getaway vehicles," Malcolm advised.

Linda laughed.

"Don't do anything I wouldn't do."

Linda started at the concern in Malcolm Brook's voice. It sounded like he really cared. She was further surprised as Malcolm seized her hand and held it close.

"I mean it Linda! I'll miss you if you wind up in the clinker."

Linda felt herself being drawn against Malcolm's body. Her heartbeat increased substantially as he pressed his lips against hers. Disappointment struck Linda as he gave her only light pressure.

"That was nice," she mused, but it was only a friendly kiss not the intimate kiss she wanted that she intuitively knew would lead to something deeper.

"I better go," she apologized. "I've got to get those ER outfits and meet the others."

"Take care," he advised. Linda blew him a kiss from the door as she left. Strong emotions were stirring up her usual calm complacency.

Later that night Turk returned to the care home with Linda, Honey Pratt, Tyler Thompson, Esther Goodenough, the Gustafsons, Frank Simpson, Art Maloney and Virgie Kelly. Turk was surprised that his Porsche and a rented, white van full of people seemed to attract little attention as they pulled into the parking lot, even with Dogzilla's head hanging out one of the windows. He guessed it was because there was so much coming and going with the construction crew.

Several of the Dog Walking Club members were dressed in ER outfits, while Frank Simpson and Virgie Kelly were dressed in formal wear. Art Maloney, the stockbroker, was wearing a business suit as was Esther Goodenough.

Turk had worked out a plan with the others. To distract the construction workers from what was happening Art and Esther were to pretend they were from the County Buildings Inspection office conducting a surprise inspection on the electrical installations. To keep the receptionist out of her space Frank and Virgie were going to pretend they had a concert date at the Care Home and had come to practice using the grand piano in the lounge next to the receptionist desk. To distract the nurses at the nursing stations on floors two to five, Gus and Tyler were showing up with their dogs, Gigi, Inuvik, Inferno and Turk's Dogzilla and pretending they were with the visiting dog program. Gloria was to remain in the van as the getaway driver and was to immediately move to the front door if called on her cell phone.

"As soon as the receptionist is distracted, Honey, Linda and I'll go up through floors two to five dressed in laundry worker's uniforms," Turk directed, "and try and spring Bea."

"Frank, and Virgie, you go into the main reception area first and insist on practising on that fancy piano of theirs."

"I'll tell them we're booked for a conference next week," the distinguished organist plotted. He took Virgie's hand as they moved toward the door.

"I'm a little scared of the consequences if we get caught," she whispered.

"Think of this as just another of our fantasies," Frank ordered. Virgie nodded and a slight smile formed on her face.

"OK dog people. Let's see if you can get the dogs up onto Floors two through five while the receptionist is busy with Frank and Virgie wanting to use the piano."

"That should start an argument," Turk continued. "While you all are distracting the receptionist, the nurses on the floors, and the construction workers, Honey, Linda, and I will go find Bea."

"Art, you and Esther go up into the construction area and pull that fake Building Inspector card I had made for you. That should distract them construction workers at the start."

Gloria moved into the van's driver's seat as the four dogs were removed for their visits.

"As soon as you spot us coming out the front door wheel the van over," Turk commanded. Gloria nodded.

"Call Tyler and have him bring down Dogzilla if anyone tries to get you out of the parking lot," Turk warned Gloria ominously, "he's trained to corner a person on command."

"I can just see the headlines now," Linda thought. "Former movie star caught as getaway driver in bizarre care home incident."

Frank and Virgie got out of the van, walked over to the front door and entered. Frank spotted the grand piano. He sauntered over to it, pulled out some music sheets from his attache case and placed them on the piano music stand. Virgie Kelly stood beside him ready to sing. Frank played an introduction and Virgie began to sing a love song from Carmen. The receptionist who was already arguing with Gus over the dog visitors suddenly jumped up and headed over to them.

"Go ahead with your visits," the receptionist yelled at Gus and Tyler. "I just wish administration would let us know about these things in advance."

Turk, Linda and Honey Pratt immediately walked through the reception area and over to the elevator. The receptionist turned but seeing people in laundry uniforms did not question their being there.

"That's lovely music but what are you two doing here?" she said to Frank and Virgie.

"We're booked for a concert next month," Frank explained. "Your Director told us it would be all right to try out the piano."

The receptionist cursed. "Nice of administration to let me know!"

Seeing the receptionist occupied, Art came through the front door with Esther.

"And who are you?" the receptionist demanded as they strode toward her. "I can't wait to find out."

Art pulled out his fake ID as a building inspector.

"You're inspecting at night?"

"We always stage one surprise inspection," Art improvised.

The receptionist looked distraught, motioned Art and Esther toward the elevator and returned to the piano area. Art and Esther went over to the elevator.

"Oh, I suppose you can practice if you want. There's

enough noise with the construction anyway. Frank broke into the opera 'Carmen' again and Virgie resumed her love song.

Art and Esther moved up to the construction area and approached the fellow who looked like he was the foreman of the construction workers. Art pulled out his fake ID card again.

"Here to inspect the electrical installation," he notified the fellow.

"The office didn't say anything about this," the foreman protested.

"Surprise inspection," Art told him.

The fellow looked displeased but led Art and Esther who pulled out an official looking notebook and pen into the area covered in plastic. The construction noise behind the plastic nearly deafened Art. He motioned the foreman to stop the workers.

"All right but be quick about it," the foreman warned. He shouted at the men to take a break for twenty minutes. The construction noise suddenly ceased and the men started filing out toward the stairs and elevator.

"That should keep the receptionist busy," Art smiled. He followed the foreman and started to take a quick look at the electrical circuits the foreman showed him.

Up on the second floor Turk had located a laundry worker placing newly laundered blankets, sheets and towels into patients' rooms. As the construction noise ceased he strode up to the fellow and asked him if he was ready for a break.

"Thanks," the laundry employee said but gave Turk a puzzled expression. "You must be new here?"

"Just started tonight," Turk improvised.

"Remember only one blanket, two sheets and one towel to each room."

"Right. Take thirty minutes if you want."

"Thanks." The employee moved off toward the elevator. Once he was ought of sight Turk motioned Linda and Honey who had ducked into one of the rooms to join him. He moved the cart down the hall with Linda and Honey and himself working the two sides of the floor.

"One blanket, two sheets, and one towel to each room." Turk instructed.

Within ten minutes all the rooms on floor two had been checked. Turk motioned them back to the elevator. He pushed the third floor button. The trio bumped into Gus and Tyler taking Gigi, Inuvik, Dogzilla and Inferno into patients' rooms.

"Not on that half," Gus pointed to part of the floor as Turk came beside him. "We've already checked."

Ten minutes later Turk was about to despair as the end of the floor was in sight. His heart thumped seconds later as Linda came out of one of the remaining rooms and motioned him over.

"Bea's in there," Linda whispered. "But she's unconscious. Must be drugged."

Turk wheeled the cart into the room. Tears filled his eyes and he placed a kiss on Bea's forehead as he realised it was indeed the former university professor. Honey joined them in the room.

"Lots of activity around here tonight," one of the floor nurses noted all the action on her floor. "Wonder why the construction guys are so quiet and Laundry has so many workers."

"What now?" Gus, Gigi and Inuvik joined the others in Bea's room. Tyler with Inferno and Dogzilla went to talk to the floor nurse.

Turk looked at the laundry cart. He motioned Honey to keep an eye out for nurses. She moved to the door and opened it a crack. Turk motioned Linda to pull the blankets out of the bottom shelf. Turk thanked God that Bea was a petite woman. He untied her restraint vest, gently pulled her from the bed, covered her with a clean blanket and then placed the remaining blankets on top of her. He smiled as there was no part of Bea showing. The trio exited the room and headed for the elevator. Tyler was still talking to the floor nurse. Gus with Gigi, and Inuvik headed in that direction. The distraction worked. The nurse bent down to pet Inuvik and the cart with Bea on it moved toward the elevator.

Inside the elevator Turk pressed the lobby button. He positioned Linda and Honey on each side of the cart in case Bea started to move. As the elevator opened piano and vocal music filled the trio's ears. Turk looked for the receptionist. She was still over at the piano listening to the music.

Turk smiled and moved the cart through the lobby with Honey and Linda still at his side. The receptionist turned but ignored them.

"Must be used to people in laundry uniforms going in and out." Turk thought to himself.

As the trio and the laundry cart reached the sidewalk the lights went on in the van and it pulled up. Turk went to the rear and opened the back. He slid the cart with Bea still on it into the back of the van. Honey, Linda and Turk climbed into the van.

Turk called Gus's cell phone, waited until it gave two rings and shut it off. The quartet waited anxiously until Gus, Tyler and the dogs came out of the front door of the care home and moved inside the van. Turk used his cell phone twice again, once to Art Maloney still looking at electrical installations with Esther and once to Frank and Virgie at the piano. He gave a nod to Gloria and she stepped on the gas and the vehicle picked up speed as it made its way out of the driveway.

"Where to?" Gloria shouted.

"My place," Turk ordered. He pulled Bea Broughton out of the laundry cart and held her tenderly in his arms.

"You're all right now, Sweetie," he informed the unconscious woman.

Gloria turned left and headed for the gated community they all lived in.

Moments later at the care home Frank Simpson stopped playing, folded up his music, placed it into his attache case and stood up.

"Thanks so much," he told the receptionist. "This piano is in remarkable shape. We'll see you again the night of the conference."

The receptionist nodded and Frank and Virgie went out the door just as Art and Esther reached it. The four of them jumped into Turk's Porsche. Frank drove them off in the Porsche without a hitch. The Construction workers who were still milling around the parking lot did not seem to suspect a thing.

At three a.m. the fourth floor nurse entered Bea's room to give her another syringe full of medicine. Her heart pounded fiercely as she encountered the empty restraint vest and bed. She shot out the door, went to the centre and pushed the emergency button. A shrill alarm bell joined the dirge of the construction sounds.

Within minutes fire department personnel and two police were at the Reception area.

"One of our patients has wandered off," the Receptionist told them. "Couldn't have gotten far even if she has somehow gotten outside. She'd be dressed only in a hospital gown and was without her cane."

"Are you sure she's not inside somewhere?"

"We're searching the whole place. Even have the construction workers searching for her."

"How in Hell could this have happened?" Dr. Jim complained to his staff the next morning. "How am I going to explain this to the family?"

"Tell them everything is being done," Dr. Jim's Head Nurse told him. "We've notified the authorities and her picture will be everywhere across the state, maybe even the country, by this afternoon."

The Dog Walking Club members were gathered in Turk O'Brien's living room. Bea Broughton had still not reached consciousness but she was showing signs of doing so. Linda Daniels and Turk were watching her closely in Turk's heart-shaped, King-Size bed.

Honey Pratt felt much warmth around her heart as Tyler Thompson sat down beside her on Turk's couch. She looked over and realised that he was no longer displaying body language that discouraged closeness. He was sitting back relaxed and gave her the welcoming smile that she had originally found so charming. He had been a perfect gentleman at the Dixieland Jazz Concert and had only insisted on a discreet kiss when dropping her back at her house.

"I want to apologize to you, Honey, for whatever it was I did that sent you into such a fury that day at the funeral parlour."

Honey stared at the Funeral Director in disbelief. The man was being downright submissive.

"He can be very nice. Maybe it is possible to win that wager."

"There's a special Dixieland Concert coming to the Opera House in New Orleans next week. Perhaps you would consider flying down and attending with me?"

Honey could not believe her ears. She was detecting pleading in the man's voice. Honey suddenly realised that a lot of her lady friend's eyes were staring at herself and Tyler. Gloria's wager came into her mind. Impulse suddenly struck the still beautiful lady. She recalled the astrological compatibility analysis that concluded that she and Tyler were likely to have an excellent and long lasting relationship. She repressed her thoughts about dating far too attractive men.

"Why thank y'all, Tyler," Honey could not believe her reply, "I'd love to attend the Dixieland Concert."

Her heart throbbed unexpectedly as Tyler's face broke into a beaming smile.

"After all, Honey rationalised, "it was good of him to come along to rescue Bea. He can't be all that bad."

"Next Tuesday morning. We'll fly direct to New Orleans and stay at my favourite hotel in the French Quarter. I'll pick you up at 6:30 a.m.?"

"I'll be looking forward to it, Sugar. Y'all really do know how to live, y'know."

"The trouble with America is that everything is run for the youth these days. We've been conditioned to believe that by the time we get to seventy or eighty years of age yet alone ninety we're going to die soon."

"Y'all don't believe that do you, Sugar?"

"I believe that every day we're given in good health late in life is a gift and that one should enjoy it to the fullest. My mother lived to over one hundred in good health and then died peacefully in her sleep. I don't see any reason why I can't do even better."

Honey realised that every person in the room was looking at Tyler Thompson with great interest. He was making them think about their own possible longevity.

Turk suddenly burst into the room.

"Bea's regained consciousness," he shouted to the assembly of dog walking friends. "Linda says she's all right, just badly frightened."

Gloria and the ladies went into the room.

"What are you going to do now, Turk?" Gus Gustafson inquired. "The police will have a full scale search going on for Bea."

"Figure her relatives will fight if she contests that 'Power of Attorney'. Think I'll just take her down to my property in Arizona for a while. Keep her safe until the heat's off."

A full scale discussion broke out amongst the men about the perils of Turk's proposed course of action. Gus Gustafson warned him that he had better not try going out of the state for some time as pictures of Bea would be all over the newspapers, at the airport, and everywhere else. Art Maloney, the stockbroker, warned Turk that Bea's extensive stock holdings would likely be sold by her son if it was thought that she had perished as under the 'Power of Attorney' he could do so.

"You're right Art," Turk acknowledged. "The bastard's already got her house for sale."

Tyler worried that the relatives should be told that Bea was still alive as soon as she was in a safe place. "What about her grandchildren, for God's sake? She's going to want to see them."

Frank Simpson warned Turk that he had better not continue to keep Bea in his house as the laundry man Turk had replaced that night might have realised something funny was going on when he was not there when he got back from his break.

"You're not exactly easy to forget," he advised the former race car driver. "Police might track you down from your description."

"What about the rental van, if someone saw it?" Tyler wondered.

"I paid cash," Frank replied. "No way they can trace it to me."

The ladies came back into the room and joined in the discussion.

"Bea's all right. She's very grateful to us for getting her out of that place," Gloria told them.

"We trying to help Turk decide what to do now," her husband replied.

Honey Pratt solved the problem for them.

"Y'all had better move Bea around from place to place for a while. You never know. Someone at that home might clue into what actually happened, particularly when they don't find her or her body."

"Bring her to my place," Tyler suggested. "No one's going to think she's hiding in a Funeral Home. But she'll need a companion. I'm out of the apartment taking care of business most of the time."

"That's very good of you, Ty," Turk O'Brien agreed.

"We'll take turns staying with her," Gloria volunteered, "starting tomorrow, first thing."

Gloria worked out a schedule for the ladies to sign up and Tyler told Turk to bring Bea over in the morning before 7:00 when his employees started turning up for work.

"I'll discuss this with Malcolm, "Gus promised. "He's got a team of lawyers that might be able to come up with a way out of this. In confidence, of course."

After the members of the dog walking group left Turk

had a long talk with Bea Broughton in his bedroom. Angus, her little Pomeranian was next to Bea on the bed. He would not let anyone remove him.

"So sorry I didn't check on you and Angus sooner," Turk confessed.

"No matter, I'm so grateful you got me out of that horrible place. And you even kidnapped Angus for me. I was so worried about him. In the times I was conscious, that is."

Bea told Turk all about her desperate attempts to escape from the place.

Turk drew Bea toward him and they embraced closely and intimately.

"Will you marry me?" Turk O'Brien asked impulsively as they disengaged. "When we're somewhere the police and border officials aren't looking for us?"

Bea nodded affirmatively. Turk pulled out a ring box from a bedside drawer and placed it on her finger.

"Brought that for you the day after we met," he confessed.

"You're such a romantic. The ring is beautiful."

Turk sighed and launched into a discussion of the possibilities the dog walking group had raised.

"I'd like to take you to my property in Arizona, but several of the group think we would be recognized on the way. They say you'll have to stay out of sight until we can manage to legally get that Power of Attorney nullified."

Tears came to Bea's eyes.

"It's your grandchildren, isn't it?"

"Yes. There must be some way we can reach a compromise with John."

"Gus says that he'll have Malcolm Brooks get his team of lawyers looking at the legal ramifications. Until then, we're going to have to keep you hidden."

"You can't know how much I appreciate that. Here's no way I'm going back to that place alive," Bea vowed.

Turk told Bea that Tyler was going to hide her in his residence above the Funeral Parlour and that he would drive her and Angus over there first thing in the morning. Bea agreed and Turk gave her a kiss on her forehead and got up to leave to give her some rest for the night.

"Please stay."

Turk could feel the fright in Bea's voice and reached for his pajamas under one of the pillows. He climbed in beside her and she positioned herself in his strong arms. Angus hung onto his place at their feet. All three of them quickly went to sleep from exhaustion.

CHAPTER 15.
Private Eye

John Broughton had difficulty drinking his coffee as he stared at a recent picture of his mother on the front page of the morning paper.

"Missing from nursing home," the headline read.

His wife Orphelia came into the dining room and John could feel his anger surging.

"How could this have happened?" he demanded. "How could the staff of the nursing home just let one of their patients just walk out the door?"

"We should sue them!" Orphelia stated. She sensed the possibility of a large settlement.

"There's something very odd about this. The Director says that they still had mother under heavy sedation. And that she's never managed to remove a restraint vest before."

"We should just sue the home, John. I'd be willing to bet they would pay a large settlement just to avoid the publicity."

John ignored his wife's words.

"There's mother's dog disappearing out of the back yard, too. And that car driving out of her driveway so early in the morning. I wonder if that man mother was with at the restaurant had anything to do with this. Do you remember his name?"

Tension shot through John's already stirred up emotions as Orphelia launched into one of her temper tantrums. She told her husband that he should be thankful that his mother and her dog had done them all a favour by disappearing. That he should speak to their lawyer immediately to transfer any remaining assets into his name and initiate a negligence suit against the care home.

"She might be lying unconscious somewhere under a tree," John complained. "It's all your fault, you're the one that convinced me that mother would be better off in that home."

"Pull yourself together John. I'll make an appointment with the lawyer today."

Bea's son felt his emotions overcoming him. A strange mixture of anger, fear, concern for his mother, irritation at his wife's unchanging avarice, and the glare of publicity that was coming at them surged through him. He decided to take a stand even if it resulted in Orphelia's temper reaching full arousal.

"I'm going to hire a private investigator," John decided in his mind. "We need to know what really happened and the truth about whoever was in the driveway that morning."

He reached for the phone. Orphelia calmed down as she heard him call their lawyer's name and went off to the kitchen.

"Lawrence," John spoke to their lawyer. "I want to hire an investigator to get to the bottom of my mother's disappearance. Do you know of anyone?"

John wrote down the name and phone number of the private investigator his lawyer had recommended. He dialled the number and set an appointment for 3:00 p.m. that day.

"I know it will be expensive," he told himself, thinking of Orphelia's anger when she learned of the additional expense. "But I have to make an effort to find her. Or at least to find out what happened."

At three o'clock John Broughton was admitted into Norm Dixon's office.

"Looks quite professional," he thought, staring at the mahogany desk, the filing cabinets and the large, middle-aged detective behind the desk.

The detective quickly grasped what John was telling him.

"You don't think your mother wandered off?"

"No. It's possible that her disappearance had something to do with a man she had met recently. An odd fellow, large and very casually dressed."

The detective drew out a pad and paper.

"Describe him more fully."

John stared at the pad as the detective picked up a drawing pencil. He gave the man some more descriptions of the man's appearance. Norm Dixon asked him several questions about his looks. Gradually the image came more and more to resemble Turk O'Brien.

"That's him," John said abruptly as the detective added the tattoo of a naked lady to his arm. "Think he must be the fellow I saw leaving mother's house at 8:00 a.m. the morning we took her to the nursing home. The car he was driving was a red Porsche."

"Do you know his name?"

"Odd name, Turkey or something like that is his first name, can't remember the second. We met him in the Tyneburst Cafe, the one down by the water."

"I'll check out that cafe and show that composite to the staff at the Care Home."

"Mother's dog disappeared out of the back yard just before she disappeared too."

"What kind of dog?"

John responded and before long the detective had a composite of Angus as well as Turk. He had the detective draw a composite of the other two dogs that had been at the restaurant. John gave him descriptions of the large Rottweiler and the Sheep Dog who had been tied to the table.

"Mother belonged to some seniors dog walking club that met regularly at the Dog Park down by the ocean."

"I'll check that out."

John instructed the detective to do everything within his power to find out exactly what had happened to his mother.

"What about money?"

John told the detective that his mother was very wealthy and to spend whatever was necessary. He gave the detective a retainer before he left the office. He had already been granted access to Bea's accounts. They shook hands and he left the office with a feeling of optimism. He decided he had better admit to his wife the action he had undertaken.

"She'll be furious!" John shuddered as he psyched himself up to deal with his wife's temper. "But I have to know what happened."

"You gave a private detective a blank cheque to investigate your mother's disappearance!" John Broughton winced several hours later as he finally found the courage to tell his wife what he had done.

"I have to know what happened to my mother."

John braced himself as Orphelia's face turned a pasty white and she launched into a full-blown temper tantrum. He waited until the volume had lessened somewhat to tell her that he wanted her to seek counselling for her anger. She choked noticeably and then went into a coughing fit. John brought her a glass of water.

"Your temper is starting to affect the children," John told

her in a soft but determined voice. He pointed at his oldest child in the living room. Tears were running down the four year old's face.

"I'm trying to establish complete financial security for us John. Goodness knows your job won't accomplish that."

John Broughton looked at his wife in amazement. It was the first time she had ever gone into a defensive position. He frowned as he knew what she said was right. He was only a substitute teacher and they were dependent on his inheritance from his mother funding their children's university education. But he was determined to find out what happened to his mother.

"The children will want to know what happened to their grandmother when they are older, Orphelia, and I want to know now."

"What happened to Granny?" John's daughter, Melissa, demanded tearfully. She was only four years of age but John realised his daughter was following every word they said.

"I'll find out," he promised, hugging the child.

Orphelia gave them both one of her deadly glares.

CHAPTER 16.
Malcolm and Monica.

Malcolm Brooks packed up his belongings in the hospital room as a nurse came to wheel him down to the exit. He felt ecstatic as his doctor had released him that morning.

"I can make it down on crutches," he offered.

"Against the rules, Mr. Brooks."

Malcolm obediently sat down in the wheelchair.

"I'll do anything to get out of here," he thought.

His butler and part-time chauffeur, Lorenzo Rodriquez, was waiting for him at the hospital door. He helped Malcolm out of the wheelchair and got him into the back seat.

"Where to Mr. Brooks?"

"Home."

Malcolm smiled as he anticipated the comfort and serenity of his large estate and looked forward to being surrounded by his large animal collection. It made him feel needed..

"Trump?"

"Picked him up this morning, Mr. Brooks."

Malcolm suddenly felt the cell phone in his pocket start to vibrate. He quickly pulled it out as the phone went into its customary musical summons.

"Hello," he wondered who was calling. Only several people had access to his private number. He was surprised to find Monica Mason on the other end. He had not seen or heard from her since his first hospitalization.

"Malcolm we've got to talk!"

"I'm just heading home from the hospital. I need a few days to recuperate, I'm afraid."

"Malcolm, I'm pregnant!"

"Pregnant?" Malcolm went into a complete panic.

"The doctor says I'm about three and a half months into the pregnancy."

Malcolm groaned to himself. Three and a half months ago was about the time he took Monica to Las Vegas for a holiday.

"But we were using birth control."

"The Doctor says it must have failed."

Malcolm tried to calm himself. He panicked but then remembered that all he had for an heir to his business was Lorne. He was convinced that Lorne would destroy the business in six months if he was given total charge. Malcolm suddenly realised that perhaps Monica having a baby was a good thing. He acknowledged that one of the greatest disappointments of his life was not having children.

"But with Monica? And at his age?"

"I'll have to get an abortion. This will ruin my career chances. I was just beginning to move forward."

Malcolm felt an even greater panic strike him. He was a lapsed Catholic but still considered an abortion the worst possible choice to the problem. He made an instant decision.

"No Monica! I'll come right over. Stay calm. We need to discuss this."

Malcolm told Lorenzo that something had come up. He redirected him to a jewelry store. Malcolm started to go into the store but felt quite fatigued over the latest crisis. He handed Lorenzo one of his credit cards, handed it to his employee and instructed him to go into the store and purchase an expensive engagement ring. When Lorenzo came back Malcolm stared at the ring in the box he had handed him.

"Great. A huge diamond. Monica will be pleased." He directed Lorenzo to go to Monica Mason's residence.

Monica met him at the door as he limped in with his crutches. Lorenzo remained in the car. Malcolm could tell that Monica had been weeping profusely. Her contact lenses were missing and dark circles were evident under his eyes. He sat down rather heavily in one of Monica's armchairs.

"Don't worry Monica. We'll get married," he promised.

Monica stared at him in complete amazement. She came over to the armchair, sat down in his lap and kissed him with great enthusiasm.

"I didn't think you cared, Malcolm."

Malcolm kept his real feelings to himself.

"I've always wanted children," he managed.

Malcolm managed to convince himself in his mind that he was doing the right thing.

Monica went bananas over the large diamond as Malcolm had thought she would.

"I want to go back to my career once the baby is born," Monica insisted.

"Of course," Malcolm readily agreed. "We'll hire a nanny. And I'll be around more to look after the baby. I need to cut back on my hours, anyway."

"What about a honeymoon?"

"A world cruise. I'll arrange it."

Monica threw herself into Malcolm's arms again.

CHAPTER 17.
Care Home Investigation.

Norm Dixon could not believe that the Director of the Care Home would not let him interview his staff nor show them the composite of the man John Broughton suspected might have something to do with his mother's disappearance. The Director quickly ended his interview and was accompanying him to the door himself.

"You realise your client is suing us for negligence?"

"That explains it! No wonder that man is downright defensive," Norm thought to himself. "Maybe this home had something to do with the woman's disappearance. But why would John Broughton hire me to find his mother if he stands to gain a large settlement by blaming the home. He should have told me they were suing the home."

Norm Dixon decided that he would have to find a way to talk to the staff despite the Director's edict.

Later that night he came back to the care home.

"Hope he's not put out a memo to his staff to keep quiet about the disappearance," he thought. He decided that a bold approach was the right way to go. He walked right through the front door and went up to the receptionist. He pulled out his identification.

"Here about the disappearance of Bea Broughton."

The middle-aged detective breathed a sigh of relief as the receptionist did not show any sign of apprehension. She pointed out the window to the woods in the distance.

"She must be lying out there in those woods somewhere. This is the second time that the local police have been incompetent. They don't seem to be able to find anyone, any more."

"This has happened before?"

"Two years ago. A male, Alzheimer's patient. Never did turn up. That's when we moved the most deteriorated patients up to the sixth floor."

Norm pulled out the composites that John Broughton had made.

"Ever seen this man?"

"No, but that huge Rottweiler looks familiar."

The detective started in surprise. He pulled out the composite of the large dog.

"This dog? Wherever did you see him?"

"The night the woman disappeared. Several dogs and their two handlers were here. Said they were part of the Visitor Dog Program. He was one of them, I swear."

Norm's intuition told him that he was on to something. The hair stood up on the back of his neck. He asked for the name of the Coordinator of the Visitor Dog Program.

"Don't know. Didn't even know that we had a program. But the administration never tells us night staff what's going on."

"How would I find out?"

"Call the Administration Office. In the morning."

The Detective asked if anything else unusual happened the night Bea disappeared. His sixth sense kicked in as the receptionist told him about all the comings and goings that night, including the dog visitors, the surprise inspection of electrical wiring, a couple practising on the grand piano for a forthcoming concert and an unusual number of people in the laundry crew.

"Mind if I go up and ask some more of the night staff about that night."

"Go right ahead. Try the third floor staff. That's where the woman disappeared from."

Norm went through to the elevator and pressed the button for the third floor. He located the floor nursing station and went over to it. He identified himself and let the nurse know he was investigating the patient disappearance case. Norm showed the composites of the man and the Rottweiler to the floor nurse.

"That dog," the nurse decided. "He was part of the Dog Visiting Program that night. Him, a Rhodesian Ridgeback, a big poodle, and a Malemute."

"You're sure?"

"Either him or a dog that looked just like him."

Norm Dixon was ecstatic. He thanked the nurse and went on to interview the rest of the staff. By the time he was through he had descriptions of the two people inspecting the electrical installations, the two people practising on the grand piano, and the identification of the man in John Broughton's composite as a laundry worker who had only been seen that night.

"Now if I can just find out who these people are." He drove off to the Tyneburst Cafe. Norm went up to the manager and pulled out a composite of the large man.

"Don't know his name," the manager dashed his hopes, but the fellow comes in all the time. 'With that dog." He pointed at the composite of the large Rottweiler. And once he had a Sheep Dog with him. Norm realised he was going to have to keep the Tyneburst Cafe under surveillance.

The next morning his suspicions were confirmed as the clerk in the administration office informed him on the phone that the care home did not have a visiting dog program nor did they have an upcoming concert lined up for their patients. The City Hall representative stated that they definitely did not schedule inspections for night time. By late afternoon not even a word of protest about his unauthorized visit had reached the detective and he concluded that the Director, the home administration office people, and its night staff were not communicating adequately with each other.

The detective's trained mind told him that an organized group of people must have removed Bea Broughton from the care home that night. Suddenly a hunch struck him.

"Maybe members of that Seniors dog walking club she belongs to?"

He picked up the phone and called John Broughton. He got through on the second ring and told him that there had been a series of unusual incidents at the care home the night his mother disappeared. He filled in the details as his client listened with great interest.

"Do you know the names of any of the dog walkers in the club your mother belongs to?"

Norm felt great disappointment as John replied in the negative but his spirits picked up again as he let him know where the seniors met.

"Down by the ocean where the river runs into the sea."

"Serenity Cove?"

"Yes, I think that's where they meet."

Norm felt his adrenaline surge as he now at least had a hypothesis to proceed on.

"The Detective thinks Mother is out there somewhere," John reported to his wife. "And that the members of her dog walking club might have had something to do with her disappearance."

"Ridiculous!" Orphelia shouted. "That detective is just setting you up for big bucks."

"What if he's right?"

"Then we'll be ruined financially, John. Or we'll have to get the Detective to get your mother back into that nursing home before she's able to run off somewhere if she hasn't already."

"Run off somewhere?"

"Out of the country. We wouldn't have the right to bring her back."

"You want her back in that home despite what happened?"

"It's in our best interest, John!"

CHAPTER 18.
New Orleans.

Honey Pratt sighed with nostalgia as Tyler Thompson came into the suite he had rented for her at his favourite hotel in the French Quarter. The smell of magnolias was coming through the open windows and the bright sunlight was luring everyone out onto the excitement filled sidewalks of the French Quarter.

"I'm not sure why I left here. I feel like I've come home at last."

"Oddly enough, I always feel the same way when I come here."

Honey stared at the handsome gentleman in the latest of Armani designed casual wear. Her heart beat increased and she felt warm vibrations around her heart as Tyler complimented her on her light cotton, very becoming outfit.

"Y'all must have lived here in a past life," Honey pronounced.

"In that case I wonder if I was the slave or the master?"

"I think you were the butler, Sugar," Honey said as she received the psychic impression of a tall, distinguished looking, tuxedo-wearing black man of about sixty years of age. His clothes were of the Abraham Lincoln era.

"Funny you should say that. I often have the feeling I've been in some of these alleys and historic buildings before. Particularly the old mansions along St. Charles Street."

"We've all been around a long time Sugar. We keep getting recycled, you know."

"But don't remember our past lives?"

"Exactly."

"In that case we had better enjoy ourselves now before we head off for the recycling process again. Heaven knows where we'll land up next time."

Honey laughed deeply. Tyler took her in his arms and kissed her passionately. Honey felt herself responding in kind. Within minutes both were lying on the replica of a Lincoln-era, canopy-covered bed.

"His energy is delicious," Honey said to herself as vibrations caressed her vagina and heart. Pictures of herself as a housekeeper on a plantation flowed into her mind.

"We've been together before," Honey assured her latest lover quite some time later as he brought her to a full, heart expanding climax. It had been as if they had known each other for eternity. Tyler groaned as his own sensuality reached its peak and the two of them clung to each other in ecstasy.

"What took you so long to find me?" Tyler complained as they finally pulled themselves out of the luxurious bed.

"You must have landed too far North this time, Sweetie."

The phone rang shrilly breaking their mood. Tyler handed Honey the phone.

'Charlotte, what you doing Girl, calling me this soon?" Honey demanded.

"I told y'all I'd call this evening."

Tyler laughed discreetly in the background as Honey promised her daughter that they would stay out of the hot sun, wear sun screen and a large hat at the race track they were going to shortly.

'Role reversal?" he questioned as Honey finally placed the

receiver in its place after assuring Charlotte that they would be having an early night as the sunshine and fresh air were sure to tire both of them out.

"I've got reservations to the midnight show at the Preservation Hall," Tyler protested. "Pete Fountain and traditional Dixieland at its best."

"That girl! She just doesn't need to know how well we're getting acquainted," Honey laughed. "Let her think we're a couple of washed-up has-beens, romantically, of course. Thinks I'm going to embarrass her in front of all the people she knows in New Orleans."

"Of course she's right!"

"Let her find out later," Honey laughed.

The two of them left for the race track, laughing and in each others arms.

"Next time let's try Tantric sex," Tyler suggested.

Honey went into shock.

"Y'all know about Tantric sex?"

"I've been researching. Some of your New Age principles seem possible to me, somehow, since I met you."

"Researching with whom?" Honey demanded. A intense surge of jealousy went flying through he mind. Tyler laughed.

"Not with a live person. I just looked the subject up on the Internet."

Honey relaxed.

"Seems perfect for older people. As I'm sure you know, it takes us longer for the blood flow to return to the genitals after a climax. Sometimes a matter of several days. We might as well do something like Tantric sex in the meantime."

"Y'all is thinking more and more like I do all the time, Sugar."

'And Tantric sex is all about blending the energy of the two people, losing themselves in the Divine, right?"

Honey stared at Tyler in absolute amazement. By this time they had reached Bourbon Street and the cab that Tyler had ordered ahead. As they sat down in the rear seat Honey pulled Tyler against him and kissed him passionately. As they relaxed several minutes later Honey gave him the first in a series of instruction on conducting Tantric sex. She told him that first they would both undress and assume a meditation position on the rug in her suite near the African statue of fertility that was on one of the end tables. Then they would stare into each others eyes until they started to lose themselves in each other. Then she would show him how to ground through the first chakra or energy centre near the tailbone. From there Honey told him they would stimulate each of their chakras in turn until they reached the sixth centre. From there hopefully they would enter the sacred space of the seventh and commune with the Divine.

Much later that night, following the race track and the Preservation Club Tyler insisted on Honey keeping her promise to teach him about Tantric sex. Honey placed her comfortable bed quilt on the floor in front of the African statue of fertility. She showed him the standard meditation position for Tantric sex and had him running energy through his seven psychic centres until they both seemed to go into a deep sleep simultaneously. Honey and Tyler spent the rest of the night and part of the morning quite comfortable snuggled in each other's arms until the phone rang shrilly. They both ignored it but it kept ringing. Honey finally staggered up and grabbed it.

"Girl, what are y'all doing calling me this early in the morning?" she demanded angrily. Tyler started laughing discreetly..

"Oh, it's noon. Uh, what are we doing today Tyler?" Honey covered up the phone.

"Thought we would take in all the varieties of jazz down here at the various clubs. You know, Big Band, Fusion, Avant Garde, Neoclassical, the Blues and Swamp."

"Swamp?"

"Rock and roll with a touch of Cajun."

Honey took her hand off the phone speaker and told her daughter that they would be having quite a quiet day since it was Sunday.

"A tour through the old mansions on St. Charles Street followed by the evening Church service at the cathedral."

Tyler went into convulsions as Honey told her daughter not to phone too late as she would be turning in early and hung up the receiver.

CHAPTER 19.
Birthday Party.

Dogzilla, Trump, Gigi, Bookkeeper, Inferno and Inuvik frolicked with each other in the ocean off the Dog Walking Park. The tide was in and Gus Gustafson marvelled at the beauty of the place, even in late Autumn. A flotilla of Canada Geese swam by as though they were teasing the dogs to come after them. All five dogs crashed into the ocean and the birds took off into the blue sky quite out of reach of the dogs.

Gus found himself going over in his mind the latest developments since Bea was rescued. He realised that Gloria was visiting Bea at the Funeral Home almost every day. He gave a sigh of relief that he had managed to convince Turk O'Brien to keep a low profile in case a description of him had been given to the police by the laundry worker he had spoken to at the Care Home.

"That fellow is so stubborn," Gus thought. He thought of how Malcolm had his team of lawyers working on some solution to the problem and hoped sincerely they would come up with one soon. Gus stared at Art Maloney who was standing with Gus watching his Greyhound, Bookkeeper, swim about with the other dogs. He noted that Tyler Thompson had both his dog Inferno and Turk's dog Dogzilla with him.

Trump was now equipped with a remote electric collar and Gus was holding on to the remote in case the large Sheep Dog showed signs of his customary harassing of Gigi.

"Dogs don't stand a chance of disobeying now," Gus concluded as he pressed the warning button on the remote. Trump must have heard the beeping because he quickly moved away from Gigi. "Smart of Turk to obtain that device for me."

Loud barking alerted Gus, Tyler and Art to the fact that they were no longer alone. Linda Daniel's Doberman, Cleo, and Pegasus, Esther Goodenough's Wheaton Terrier, joined Gus as their mistresses reached him. Gus noted that Esther was using an electric leash and that Pegasus no longer was pulling her along. She removed the leash leisurely and Pegasus joined the other dogs in the water. He noticed Art Maloney give the former flight attendant a kiss and a warm embrace.

"Missed my chance," he laughed to himself, thinking of Gloria's wager.

Gus noted a trace of sadness in Linda Daniel's eyes as she watched Art embrace Esther.

"She's got the hots for Malcolm," he guessed. "Or maybe it's just Gloria's wager. Actually I wonder what's up with Malcolm. I haven't seen him since he got out of the hospital. Guess he's taking care of his horse racing problems." Gus decided to help Linda's cause.

"Gloria and I are holding a party next Friday for Malcolm," he improvised. "It's his eightieth birthday. Will you join us, Linda? And the two of you as well?" he invited Esther and Art. "It's a surprise party."

Art and Esther nodded in agreement as did Linda.

"Quite an adventure the other night," Art Maloney said exuberantly for him.

"You've got quite a talent as an imposter," Linda joked..

A week later Linda Daniels drove up to Gus and Gloria's sprawling bungalow with trepidation. She wondered if Malcolm's increased attention to her while he was in the hospital was any indication he was viewing her as anything more than a close friend. She had not heard anything from him since his release. She remembered her deep disappointment when she had turned up at the hospital only to find him gone. He had not sent her a message.

"He's so egotistical," she mused. "He thinks of no one but himself. No wonder his wife left him."

The driveway was already full of cars and Linda had to back out onto the road to park.

A crowd of dog walking club members was spread all over the inside pool and living room area. Linda noticed an empty chair beside Honey Pratt and Tyler Thompson and idled over.

"How was New Orleans?" she said to the newly returned duet.

"The jazz concerts were wonderful," Honey told her as Tyler greeted Linda warmly and then moved to give Gloria a hand with circulating the appetisers, "but my daughter is having a fit. Want's to know why I'm dating a Caucasian and showing him off to all her friends in New Orleans."

"Really?"

"Not only that, she's concerned about Tyler's age. Thinks I'm losing it completely. Honey gave a quick summary of her daughter's objections.

Honey said that her daughter had told her that she was losing it big time. That dating Tyler was just asking for pain at his eventual death. Honey told Linda that she had retaliated by saying that Tyler was not like an older, rescue dog from a Dog Pound with a very limited number of years. That humans had a good chance now of living until they were at least a hundred.

"You mean you told her that Tyler was not a rescue senior?" Linda choked.

"Exactly, and that he and I had a lot in common like love of dogs, the same brand of Bourbon, Dixieland Jazz, and New Orleans, not to mention that his Sun in Capricorn trine my own Moon in Taurus is one of the best astrological compatibility signs."

Linda laughed.

"How did you find that out?"

"An Astrology compatibility analysis, Sugar. I don't enter any relationship without one now."

"Maybe that's where I went wrong. I should have had one of those done years ago."

"Good thing that Charlotte assumes that my relationship with Tyler is platonic. Doesn't think a man his age can still get it on. If she knew what really went on down in New Orleans it would be she having the personality fracture not me."

"You're not going to tell her?"

"Y'all think I'm crazy, Sugar. That girl would have the rest of my family up here trying to get me back to what they think is my normal state of mind."

Linda laughed as Honey related how she had lied to Charlotte for the second time when she had phoned down late one evening as Tyler and she had just got back from the large New Orleans cemetery and they were changing clothes to head out again to do some more dancing at the famous Preservation club.

"Told her I was retiring early for the night as the country air had tired Tyler out. She was only too eager to believe me."

"Knowing Tyler the exact opposite was occurring, wasn't it?"

"You're right on Sugar."

Their conversation ceased as Gus Gustafson shouted "Quiet, he's coming!" Everyone turned toward the front door.

As it opened, Monica Mason came through followed by an unusually well dressed Malcolm Brooks on crutches. Linda's mouth flew open in astonishment. She felt considerable pain around her heart as her romantic illusions faced the light of reality.

"He must have called her," she thought. "The moment he got out of the hospital. Linda felt like someone had struck her in the stomach. Her cheeks turned bright red and she felt two inches high.

"I wonder what's wrong with me," she thought. "How could I think I could possibly compete with Malcolm's usual dates."

"Surprise," everyone in the place yelled. Linda wished she could be anywhere but in Gus Gustafson's living room.

Linda noted that things were getting worse. Malcolm was heading straight in her direction guiding Monica toward her.

"Linda, you remember my girl friend Monica," he said gruffly.

"Who is Linda?" Monica demanded.

"You remember. You met her at the hospital. Linda is the veterinarian that keeps Trump and the rest of my animal menagerie in good health."

"Oh, of course, the animal attendant."

Linda forced herself to put out her hand as the much younger woman put out hers. Linda noted with a very sick feeling that Monica was wearing an engagement ring. Her heart felt like several swords were piercing it. Her eyes went down to the young woman's waist. Linda realised it had expanded considerably.

"She's pregnant! That explains it."

"Malcolm and I are engaged," Monica told her.

"He doesn't even know that I am attracted to him," Linda

realised with increasing pain. "It isn't like he was deliberately trying to wound me."

"Congratulations," she managed to gasp. Honey Pratt put a empathetic hand to her shoulder.

"Isn't it great! Malcolm is taking me on a world cruise on our honeymoon."

"Happy Birthday to you," Linda welcomed Gus Gustafson coming into the room with a huge birthday cake with eight lines of candles burning on it. Everyone started singing. Linda breathed a huge sigh of relief as Malcolm and Monica moved toward the well-stocked table and the cake.

Malcolm took a huge intake of breath and attempted to blow out the candles. He managed all but five and quickly exterminated them in another breath. Gus reached for a bottle of champagne and poured Malcolm and Monica the first drinks. They drank it rather quickly.

"Too quickly," Linda thought.

Everyone was congratulating Malcolm on his birthday and engagement. Linda could see her old friend enjoying the party a little too much. She frowned as his nephew, Lorne Brooks, was present at the party and kept refilling Malcolm's glass every time it emptied. She could see Lorne glaring at Monica occasionally when he thought she was not looking.

"She's ruining his inheritance plans," Linda realized.

'I don't like Malcolm drinking like that," Linda thought. "And I hope he's not going to drive after all those drinks." Linda watched as Malcolm continued to click glasses and drink down the champagne Lorne poured for him. The party goers were giving him and Monica well wishes.

Gus came over and gave Linda a hug of sympathy.

"You all right?"

Linda shook her head. She felt herself under extreme

emotional stress and moved toward the door. She bumped into Lorne Brooks on the way.

"Leaving so soon?" Lorne demanded as Linda moved past him.

Linda noted that Lorne had a camera around his neck and was furiously taking pictures of Malcolm and Monica in between refilling Malcolm's champagne glass. He had an obsessed look in his eyes.

"Sick animal at my office," Linda lied. By the time she had gotten her SUV halfway down the road Linda was trying to shut out her pain and trying to laugh at herself for even daring to think of trying again to attract Malcolm's romantic interest.

"He's out of my league," she decided.

Her Doberman, Cleo, greeted her warmly as she went into her house. "I had best restrict myself to animal companions," Linda decided. "Dogs are more dependable, loyal to their owners and less complicated anyway."

Thoughts of Malcolm would not stay out of her mind. Linda pulled out her tranquillizer case and stared at the pills. Linda shook her head as she realised what she was going to have to do. She was going to have to follow Honey Pratt's advice and not see him anymore. Linda decided to resign as Malcolm's veterinarian. Linda managed to summon up her will power. She went into the kitchen and flushed her tranquillizers down the drain.

"I'm never going to become a drug addict," she vowed.

"I've got to stop seeing Malcolm," her mind told her. "Surely I'll eventually stop thinking about him."

Several hours later Malcolm staggered out to his Cadillac. Lorne Brooks and Monica Mason were with him.

"You better drive, Lorne," Malcolm ordered.

"What's the matter? You getting old? Can't hold your liquor anymore?"

Malcolm looked at Monica.

"You drive?"

Monica staggered noticeably. Malcolm realised she was physically having trouble with the pregnancy. Considerable nausea and a draining of her energy.

"Never mind."

Malcolm made a monumental effort to force his eyes to focus. He opened the car door and sank down into the driver's seat. Lorne helped Monica around to the passenger side and got her into her seat belt. He went into the back seat.

Malcolm started the car. He slowly moved out of the driveway narrowly missing Frank Simpson's Mercedes in the process. Malcolm stared at the white line. There seemed to be two of them. Malcolm cautiously pulled the car into the side of the road.

"There's no way I should drive." He removed the keys and tried to hand them to his nephew in the back seat.

"What's the matter Malcolm? You getting old or something?"

"Show him Malcolm!" Monica demanded.

Malcolm sighed and pulled the car back onto the road again. He made it down two side streets but when he went to pull onto the freeway to drive Lorne home his coordination was not up to it. He missed the final turn onto the freeway, went off onto a grassy area off the shoulder and crashed into a tree.

"Did you hear the bad news about Malcolm?" Linda was surprised to hear Honey Pratt ask as they met the next morning at the dog walking park.

"What news?" Honey handed her the morning paper.

"Millionaire arrested for DUI." Linda looked at the

picture under the headline. Malcolm was looking much less than his dignified self as some cameraman had captured a shot of him and Monica inside his luxury Cadillac. The Cadillac was resting against a tree next to the freeway. Linda noticed that the windshield was cracked and Monica had blood on her face. She was wearing an extremely angry expression.

"Oh my God! He must be mortified," Linda exclaimed.

"He didn't injure his leg again did he?"

"Just his pride," Honey laughed.

"I hope that doesn't cause complications with the baby."

CHAPTER 20.
Termination.

You're terminated Lorne," a furious Malcolm Brooks informed his nephew as his Senior Vice President, Reg Sanderson, looked on in agreement. "You'll find that we've given you a very generous retirement pension."

Lorne stared around his uncle's comfortable and impressive office and then at his uncle in complete astonishment.

"But it's you that got plastered all over the morning newspaper."

Malcolm angrily told him that he had called an old friend at the newspaper that morning to find out the name of the cameraman who took the picture. That he had been curious because no one had seemed to be around the car after he hit the tree and the police had been rather slow to arrive.

"My friend told me in confidence that you were the one that sent the picture by courier in time for the deadline."

Lorne's face suddenly went completely white. He turned away from Malcolm and looked at Reg Sanderson in shock.

"What about Malcolm? He's the one that should be terminated. Driving under the influence; knocking up a young woman. You want a CEO who shows such poor judgement?"

"Let it go, Lorne," Malcolm felt his anger dissipating. He was thinking of his brother's wife and the pain she would experience if she knew the truth about her son.

"The announcement will say only that you requested an early retirement," Reg Sanderson assured Lorne.

Malcolm sighed as tears came into his nephew's eyes.

"I'm sorry, Lorne. There's nothing else I can do. I demand loyalty at the very least from my top executives."

"You bastard!" Something snapped in Lorne's mind. He sprang at Malcolm and grabbed him by his suitcoat. He started to swing at Malcolm with his right hand. Malcolm grabbed his arm in mid motion and expertly put it into an armlock. Lorne went down onto his knees and broke into tears.

"Take Lorne back to his office and help him pack up, will you Reg?"

The Senior Vice President nodded and pulled Lorne up from the floor. He led Malcolm's nephew toward the closed door.

"I'll make you pay for this!" Lorne shouted. Reg Sanderson opened the door and pushed the distraught man through. He closed the door.

Malcolm picked up the phone and punched in some numbers.

"Security, get me Mitchell."

"Keep an eye on my nephew Lorne, will you Mitch. I've just terminated him and he's making threats. Have one of your people follow him for a few days. I think he'll be all right but I want to make sure. Great, you'll take care of it yourself. I appreciate that."

Malcolm put down the phone, then thought better of it.

He punched in another extension.

"Law Department, this is Malcolm Brooks, put me through to Jason."

"Jason, you've seen the morning papers. Yes, very unwise of me. I'll enter a guilty plea and take whatever the court decides. I deserve it."

"You'll take care of the matter personally. My appreciation. Keep me up to date on the happenings."

Malcolm sighed deeply as he put down the phone. He buzzed his executive secretary, Jessica. She came right in immediately.

"Jessica, I'm going home. Reg will fill in until I'm back."

"Yes, Mr. Brooks."

Malcolm got up and moved out of the room using his crutches. He felt the impact of his age fully for the first time.

"I'd better see how Monica's making out. I know the animals make her nervous when she's at my estate."

He drove directly home trying to shut thoughts of Lorne's mother out of his mind. As he drove through the gate of his estate he wondered at the number of automobiles in his driveway. Fire trucks, an ambulance and several police cars were parked and people seemed to be searching through his gardens and woods.

Malcolm flew through his front door and found his housekeeper trying to calm a hysterical Monica in his living room. She was sobbing uncontrollably. Malcolm braced himself with his crutches as Monica stood up, ran over to him and threw herself against him.

"What happened?" Malcolm questioned his housekeeper.

"I'm so glad you're here, Mr. Brooks. It's Raptor, your boa constrictor. Trump lunged at his cage and broke the glass door somehow. Raptor got out and he and Trump got into a wrestling match. It scared Miss Mason when she came across them slithering around the living room and when she tried to run out the front door the big snake and the dog followed her."

Malcolm groaned.

"I told you Raptor was defanged, Monica. He's harmless."

Malcolm dislodged Monica back into an armchair, went into the kitchen and made some Camomile tea. He went into his bar and poured a double whiskey for himself.

"Drink this!" he ordered Monica. "It will calm you."

"The snake tried to wind around me, Malcolm," Monica sobbed. She gulped the tea down. "And I want you to get rid of that awful dog."

"For Heaven's sake, Monica. You're a grownup. Raptor isn't that powerful. All you have to do is grab him by the tail or the head and pull him off. Now you've got half the neighbourhood up in arms. And getting rid of Trump is not on the asking block."

Malcolm's lack of sympathy seemed to enrage the young woman. She aimed the now empty tea cup and threw it at him at close range. The cup hit Malcolm on the head and shattered into several pieces. Malcolm's crutches gave way and he crashed to the floor. Malcolm's housekeeper rushed to his aid and his pet Howler monkeys in a large cage in the glassed in porch near the living room started to whoop.

The housekeeper got Malcolm into a chair and started to blot the blood running from a cut on his forehead.

"Our engagement is off," Monica shouted at him just as the front door opened and Malcolm's butler staggered in with Raptor coiled around him. Monica screamed. The butler seemed unfazed and moved over to Raptor's glass cage and peeled the big snake off himself. It moved with a fluid motion back onto its favourite wooden perch. The butler placed a sheet of plywood across the door of the cage.

"That should hold him."

Monica pulled the large, diamond ring off her left hand and fired it at Malcolm. It struck him on the chest and bounced down onto the floor. Malcolm's housekeeper gathered up the large ring and handed it to Malcolm.

"Where did you find Raptor?" Malcolm questioned his butler.

"He was heading for Mrs. Gustafson's house, I think, sir. After her Siamese cat again, I bet. He was almost to the house when I spotted him."

"That's all you care about, that horrible snake?" Monica headed for the door.

"I'll drive you, Monica." Malcolm offered.

"Over my dead body. I'll see you in court! I'm sure that accident has permanently damaged my looks." Monica went out the front door, slammed it hard and the glass shattered.

"Want me to intercept the young lady?" Malcolm's butler offered.

"Just drive her home, will you Lorenzo" Malcolm handed his butler his car keys. His housekeeper went to deal with the glass all over the floor.

"By the way, where is Trump?"

"The firemen are chasing him, Mr. Brooks. Him, your black jaguar, Diego and your Cassowary Bird, Razor. But don't worry, they are all still inside the estate grounds."

"How did Diego and Razor get out?"

"Rushed past their attendant, Mr. Brooks, when he opened their gate and was distracted by all the firemen crashing through the grounds. But don't worry the firemen are tracking them by their radio collars."

Malcolm groaned, pulled out his cell phone and dabbed the blood on his forehead with his handkerchief.

"Law Department," he requested the receptionist at his office.

"Jason, another problem, I'm afraid."

"Yes, the planets must have gone retrograde or something, as my new age friend Honey Pratt would say. My pregnant, former fiancee is suing me. Claims her looks have been damaged by that accident. Just negotiate a settlement with her lawyer, will you? And make sure someone makes an offer today. She's rather distraught and might do something drastic. I want custody of the baby when it's born included in the agreement. I don't think Monica will resist if you offer her the right price. Keep increasing the offer if she refuses."

Malcolm hung up the phone after his lawyer assured him he would immediately take care of the matter personally.

"You need a doctor, Mr. Brooks," his housekeeper assured him, looking at the ugly cut on his forehead that was still spewing blood.

"I need more than that, I'm afraid, a psychiatrist maybe."

CHAPTER 21.
Private Investigation Continues.

Private detective Norm Dixon ignored the chilly wind blowing near the ocean and scanned the start of the dog walking park for members of the Seniors Dog Walking Club. He held the composites of Bea's dog Angus, and the man named something like Turkey that John Broughton had helped him with. He also had a photo of several of the members and their dogs he had located from the archives of the local newspaper.

"This is all I have to go on in this latest case," he muttered to himself. "That fellow hasn't turned up at the Tyneburst cafe despite all my surveillance and I still haven't found out who all those people at the care home were."

The burly detective felt quite a bit of negativity strike him as he remembered his conversation with Bea Broughton's son as he had renegotiated the fee for investigating his mother's disappearance given the recent developments. His investigative mind had detected a lot of guilt at the man's decision to place his mother in the care home.

"Odd that well-off citizens that had a lot to lose would endanger themselves to pull some deteriorated person out of a care home."

Norm put such thoughts out of his mind. "That's none of my business," he said to himself.

"I don't think that Bea Broughton is lying somewhere

under a tree," Norm Dixon mused. "And these people have something to do with it."

Norm stared at two ladies coming down the walkway with two dogs cavorting in front of them. He glanced at the names of some of the dog walking members from a photo he had found in the local community newspaper.

"My God. That's one of them all right. "Linda Daniels, the local veterinarian."

Norm intercepted the women. He started as a large Doberman barked sharply.

"Cleo, sit," one of the women ordered. Norm looked relieved as the dog sat as ordered but noticed it still stared at him in a warning fashion. He had a fear of dogs from an incident in his childhood. The smaller dog growled at him as he moved toward his owner.

The large man freaked.

"My God, it's a Pitbull. He must be picking up my fear." He aimed a kick at the dog as it continued to growl. Bourbon lunged at his shoe. Norm screamed as the dog's teeth sunk into his heel. He desperately tried to shake the dog off.

"Damn it. Do something!" he screamed.

Norm used his other foot and his considerable bulk to pin the Pitbull's head against the concrete. He managed to manoeuvre his free foot over the dog's throat and put his weight on it. The dog gasped but did not let go of his foot. A crowd of dog lovers gathered around the pair.

"Take your foot off Bourbon's throat," Norm stared at the Afro-American lady in disbelief.

"His jaws have locked!" Norm screamed. He was completely terrified and did nothing.

"That's a myth. Y'all are an idiot!"

He screamed in considerable pain as the woman drew

back her fist and punched him firmly in his large belly. He staggered but managed to keep his foot on the Pit Bull's throat. His foot was still in the dog's jaws but the animal could at least breath.

"Get off the dog's throat!" A man screamed. "A big man like you afraid of that small dog."

"Stop hurting the dog," a little old lady yelled at him. Norm was shocked as the crowd seemed to be on the side of the Pitbull. The pain in his stomach and foot were excruciating and the detective increased the pressure on the dog's throat.

Honey Pratt was having a fit.

"Bourbon can't breathe," she screamed. "Get your foot off his neck, now!"

Norm Dixon gasped with pain as the Afro-American lady suddenly charged into him again and kicked his foot off her dog's throat. He was still trying to get his breath back after the blow to his stomach. He went down to all fours with the dog's teeth still sunk into his right heel. The dog seemed unwilling to release the shoe. The detective was completely frantic.

Linda Daniels moved in, grabbed hold of the animal, and gently massaged it. Her massage worked. Suddenly the dog calmed down and spit out Norm's foot as the detective pulled his foot away. Linda gave the leash to Honey and she pulled the dog out of range of the detective. Norm Dixon staggered to his feet and tried to ignore the pain in his foot and stomach. He reached down and noticed blood seeping out of his shoe.

"Is the dog all right?" Norm was amazed as the audience did not seem to care the slightest about whether he was all right.

"This is a Dog Park." Some man yelled at Norm. "We don't put up with abuse of animals, here!"

Norm felt a lot of relief as the dog stopped gasping. The

crowd simmered down as the dog started breathing normally again.

"Don't y'all ever do that again to my dog!"

Norm Dixon decided it was in his best interest to ignore the dog's biting and the woman's violence. He tried to slow down his pounding heart. He was deathly afraid of dogs.

"Bourbon was trying to protect you," Linda Daniels told Honey.

"I'm sorry. It's my fault," Norm Dixon managed to gasp.

"You shouldn't have attempted to kick him," Linda Daniels exclaimed.

"You're right." Norm ignored the pain and took the blame rather than antagonize the women and the crowd further.

"Whatever do you want, anyway?"

"Are you two friends of Bea Broughton?" Norm's trained eye noticed a startle reaction as both ladies took a closer look at him.

"Yes," the younger woman finally replied. "A lovely lady, Bea. She's disappeared, you know, from a care home."

"That's what I wanted to talk to you about."

Norm Dixon pulled out the composite pictures that he and John Broughton had made.

"Does either of you know who this might be? Or who these dogs belong to?"

The detective's trained eyes took in the sharp intake of breath from the woman with the Pitbull. The other woman looked more closely at the composite of a large man dressed in casual clothes and shook her head.

"That little dog looks just like Bea Broughton's Pomeranian, Angus." Linda Daniels thought fast. The composite of the man was remarkably like Turk O'Brien. It was complete with a large tattoo of a naked lady on his right arm.

"Who are you?"

Norm pulled out his identification.

"A private detective. I'm working for Bea Broughton's son. He's determined to get to the bottom of his mother's disappearance."

"A sad thing that! I don't know why she was ever put into that home. There's nothing wrong with Bea's mind."

The detective felt the hair on his neck standing up. He sensed the woman might be right. Others had told him the same thing. Norm Dixon noted that Linda Daniel's tone of voice sounded sincere.

"That's none of my business," he told himself.

"I'm afraid we can't help you. We're in a hurry to get to a pet store."

The detective nodded and let the ladies go on toward the parking lot. He sighed deeply as the crowd dispersed, still glaring at him, and forced himself to ignore his pain. The ladies had told him more than they knew.

"They know something they're not telling me," he decided. He took off his shoe and placed a handkerchief around his bleeding heel. He forced his pounding heart from his fear of dogs to slow down. Then he forced himself to ignore the pain of the bite and scanned the walkway looking for more members of the Seniors' Dog Walking Club.

Five minutes later adrenaline shot through Norm Dixon's system as a large, white, Standard Poodle came into view running beside a Malemute.

"Those dogs. They're like two of the four visiting dogs that the care home nurse described." Norm's eyes bugged out of his face. He stared at the man walking with the dog and checked out the photo of the dog walking club members.

"Gus Gustafson!" The detective moved to intercept the man. "A movie producer of all things."

This time a huge Malemute blocked his way as he strode over to the dog's owner. The dog was not growling but kept himself between the detective and his master. Norm Dixon felt his fear of dogs choking his breath again. He tried to suppress his anxiety but when the large white poodle rushed up, stood on her hind legs and placed her paws on his chest he lost it.

"Put those dogs on a leash. Get them away from me," he shouted.

"He's at it again," a former member of the crowd yelled. Several of the original spectators rushed over to the scene.

"Shame! A big man like you. The poodle is trying to get you to play with her."

"To Hell with you," Gus Gustafson told him. "Don't you know this is an off-leash, dog park? They're right. Gigi is just trying to get you to play with her."

Norm Dixon managed to calm himself down a little.

"This your poodle?" He tried to stay calm as the dog seemed to think he was a play toy and jumped on him several times, growling playfully and then running backwards.

"What's it to you?"

Norm suppressed his scream as the huge Malemute growled menacingly as he moved closer to his owner. He pulled out his ID and told the man he was investigating Bea Broughton's disappearance. The dog's handler did not seem to be impressed. The crowd of onlookers watched closely. Norm realised they were watching to make sure he did not abuse another dog.

"That woman didn't deserve to be put in the care home," Gus Gustafson told the detective.

"That's their motivation," Norm Dixon realised. "They're convinced they were doing the right thing. Maybe they are right," he wondered as he remembered the look of guilt John

Broughton had exhibited when he was telling the detective what had happened.

"Not my business," the detective brushed off his own rapidly developing feelings of anxiety. He prided himself on being on the right side of justice.

"Looking for this fellow," Norm handed the man the composites of the man from the restaurant and the Rottweiler. "And his dog."

"Don't know who that is! All male Rottweilers look much the same."

"You are the owner of this poodle and the Malemute, then?"

"None of your business." Norm watched in amazement as the tall, bushy haired man called the dogs and went down the road to the parking lot without another word. Norm collapsed on one of the benches beside the walkway. The crowd dispersed again.

"Fellow knows something," he decided. "Likely one of the people that were there that night." His breathing finally returned to normal as he watched for some more members of the dog walking club. "There's a lot more here than meets the eye."

Once Gus was far enough away from the detective he pulled out his cell phone and punched in Tyler Thompson's number.

"Tyler, you've got to get the Hell out of here with Dogzilla. There's a private detective with a composite of Turk and the dog. He's intercepting people on the walkway going to the parking lot."

"Yes, use the back way. We'll meet later, at my place. Make sure there's no one following you." Gus punched in some more numbers into his cell phone.

At the same time at the parking lot Linda reached for her cell phone as it rang.

"Yes, I know. He stopped Honey and me, too. Yes, I'll warn Turk O'Brien?"

"Glad Bourbon bit that man. Dogs can sense it when someone doesn't wish you well."

Linda reached Turk O'Brien on the second ring. She alerted Bea's friend that there was a private detective circulating a composite drawing of him at the Dog Walking Park. She told him that the drawing of himself was a very good likeness.

"We need a meeting, Sugar," Honey interjected. Linda passed on the message.

"This evening. At Gus's place. I'll let the others know." Linda Daniels folded up her cell phone and placed it back into her pocket.

"Going to have to get Bea out of this area," Honey advised the veterinarian. "And Turk."

"Or we're all going to wind up in the clink,"

"Nonsense, Sugar, that fat cretin's no match for a group of seniors pooling their resources."

"I'll give the rest an hour or two to get home and then I'll call them about the meeting. Particularly Gus and Gloria since it's at their place."

An hour and a half later Norm Dixon was certain that the dog walking seniors knew something they were not telling him. Almost every one of them had shown a startled look to his trained eye when the composite of the mystery laundry worker at the Care Home had been shown to them.

"Influential people," he concluded. "And not easily intimidated. I'll have to have proof before I make any accusations."

"I had better contact John Broughton again," the detective

said to himself. "There's more than meets the eye here. I'll have to investigate further. Look's like I'm going to have to follow these seniors around. It'll cost that fellow big bucks if I have to deal with vicious dogs and their vicious owners as well as everything else. Hope he's up to it."

He limped back to his car to make an appointment with his doctor about the wound on his heel.

CHAPTER 22.
Revenge.

Monica Mason stared at Lorne Brooks in total disbelief. He was standing on her doorstep looking quite dishevelled. She had been weeping for days since Malcolm Brook's butler had driven her home and the last thing she wanted was someone named Brooks standing in her doorway. She had been arguing with herself ever since Malcolm's lawyer had called and offered her a generous settlement if she was willing to give custody of the child to Malcolm when it was born. Her own lawyer had advised her against the settlement when she had called for advice.

"We'll get more in court," he promised.

"What the Hell do you want?"

"Your lawyer called. Said you were launching a civil suit against Malcolm for damages in the accident. He wants me to testify about Malcolm being drunk."

Monica motioned Lorne into her townhouse. He sat down on one of Monica's armchairs. She was busy dabbing at her eyes.

"How come you broke up with Malcolm?"

"He's so selfish!" Monica started weeping openly. "All he cares about are those god awful, exotic pets of his."

"Oh, you mean the Jaguar and Pyrannas from South America and the Boa Constrictor from India, the Green Tree Python and giant Cassowary Bird from New Guinea, and the Howler monkeys from God knows where."

"Pyrannas, those fish in his living room are Pyrannas? Where is the Green Tree Python?"

"A good thing you didn't go for a stroll around the grounds!"

"He's impossible!" Monica went into a hysterical weeping fit again.

"There's a way we can both get even with him."

Monica was surprised at the venom in Lorne's voice.

"What did he do to you?"

"Fired me. After all I've done for him and the company!"

Monica stopped crying. She listened attentively as Lorne told her that he could arrange an abortion, even at this late date. He told Monica that Malcolm desperately wanted the child. He promised to make the arrangements, stand by her side for moral support and then connect her with an even more prestigious modelling agency that the Montgomery one.

"What agency?"

Lorne gave her the name of the most exclusive modelling agency in New York. He told her that he was a close friend of its owner.

"Or even better, you could marry me. That way, I would have control of his child, his only chance of an heir besides me. Think of it, Malcolm having to answer to me for a change, maybe even begging."

Monica stared at Lorne in horror.

"I would never marry a Brooks! Never, even if they were the last man alive. You're all weird."

"How about the abortion, then?"

"You're insane. I'm close to four months pregnant, maybe even five. Any more time and the baby might even live. That's what Malcolm's lawyer has been telling me."

"He's lying."

Monica stared at Lorne in alarm. His tone of voice was furious. His eyes were staring at her like some maniacs. Monica suddenly reached a decision. She realised her nerves were completely frayed. She realised she was not up for a contest in court.

"No, I'm going to accept the last offer Malcolm's lawyers made me," she blurted. "He gets the child and I get financial security for the rest of my life."

Monica freaked as Lorne suddenly jumped to his feet and came toward her. She could tell he was out of control. She screamed loudly as he seized her arm and pulled her up to her feet.

"You're hurting me!" Monica tried to pull free.

"You're coming with me!" Lorne insisted, dragging Monica toward the front door. She resisted and he struck her across the face.

"Don't," she screamed.

"You're getting an abortion," Lorne told her as he opened the front door. His expression turned to horror as a man was waiting on the doorstep, a gun in his hand pointing at Lorne. Lorne quickly recognized Malcolm's Head of Security.

"Mitch, it's me Lorne. Put the gun down."

"Let go of the lady, now!" Mitch motioned Lorne away from Monica. Lorne sprang toward his tormentor. Mitch clubbed him over his head with the butt of his pistol and Lorne sank down unconscious. Another man came out of a car next to Lorne's and dragged Malcolm's unconscious nephew into the back seat.

Monica was crying hysterically.

"I'm sorry, Miss Mason. Don't worry. He won't be bothering you any more."

"Who are you?"

"Malcolm Brook's Head of Security. Malcolm told us to keep an eye on his nephew."

"What will you do with him?"

"Short stay in a sanitarium," Mitch promised. "Until he stabilises."

"My God! I'll accept Malcolm's offer. Just get me out of this city."

"That's very wise, Miss Mason. It will be arranged. In the meantime one of my security guards will be watching this place."

"Thanks." Monica headed back into her townhouse. She sank down into her chesterfield and broke down in tears, sobs shaking her body..

"At least this way I can go back to my modelling career," she decided some time later. That decision seemed to calm her.

"There's no way I'm ready to be a mother."

CHAPTER 23.
Panic.

Turk O'Brien pulled into Gus and Gloria Gustafson's large driveway in his second car, a well-worn Toyota, and noted gratefully from the cars that the entire group appeared to be gathered. He pulled in next to Frank Simpson's Mercedes and made his way through the front yard area. He knocked on the front door. Gus himself opened the door and Turk moved into the impressive house. Turk found himself looking out glass windows stretching to the raised ceiling and staring out at an impressive panoramic ocean view.

"You and Bea are going to have to get out of this area for a while," Art Maloney advised him.

"You're sure this composite looks like me?"

"Damn sure!" Gus reinforced Art's opinion. He's got composites of Angus and Dogzilla, too. The others nodded.

"Not just out of this area," Esther warned.

Malcolm Brooks warned Turk that his lawyers had advised that the only place that would be safe from interference was Mexico or some other foreign country once he and Bea went ahead with their plans to get lawyers to contest the Power of Attorney. That if it became known that Bea was still alive then anywhere within the United States Bea would be subject to US law and Turk would be risking arrest as a kidnapper, and the rest of them as accomplices.

"I'd have to cross two states and an international border to reach Mexico," Turk sighed. He was becoming weighed down with worry about Bea.

"There might be a way," Tyler suggested.

"I'll do anything," Turk vowed.

Tyler launched into an explanation of his shipments to Mexico of finished coffins for Mexican funeral homes. He explained that he was in partnership with a chain of Mexican funeral homes and part of his responsibility was the supplying of coffins of the highest quality wood. Tyler told them that every four months he arranged the shipping of twenty or so coffins in two of his trucks all the way from his funeral home to a funeral home in Guadalajara, Mexico. He added that a shipment was scheduled in the next two weeks. Everyone in the room figured out what he was suggesting at once.

"It might work," Gus Gustafson was the first to speak.

"I'll accompany the shipment personally as usual," Tyler volunteered. "Providing Honey, here, will accompany me."

Honey Pratt gasped. She realised that the Funeral Director was trapping her into remaining in his life, at least until Bea and Turk could safely reach Mexico. She realised her daughter was going to have convulsions at the thought of her heading off to Mexico with Tyler. She also realised that she had become much too fond of Tyler.

"I'll be just like Linda," Honey thought to herself. "Ty'll say he just wants to be a friend one of these days and I'll go around with a broken heart for the rest of my life."

"I'll have to go," Honey decided. "I'm not ready yet to cope with losing Tyler. But maybe it will be all right to tell Charlotte that I'm taking a trip to Mexico with Tyler. The girl still thinks our relationship is platonic."

"Yes, it just might work. Of course, your regular crew will have to be replaced unless you feel they would cooperate and can be trusted," Esther Goodenough added more plotting to the plan. "But maybe a couple of the club members could drive the trucks in their place."

"I'll do it," Malcolm Brooks volunteered. "I was going to take a vacation anyway."

Linda Daniels gave him a look of absolute astonishment. It was the first time she had seen him since his arrest for drunk driving. She tried to still the ache in her heart as his voice continued to do something to her. He had not even called when her partner, another veterinarian, had notified him of the change in veterinarians.

"Providing Linda will come along and keep an eye on Trump. I wouldn't want to leave him behind."

"That's all he wants," Linda mused when she got over her shock. "A caretaker for Trump." But Linda could not believe that Malcolm was becoming so altruistic he was volunteering several weeks of his time to help someone he hardly knew and that he wanted her to accompany him.

"Maybe Monica will look after Trump," she suggested.

Malcolm gave a short, rueful laugh.

"Monica is not speaking to me! Broke our engagement after Raptor coiled around her. Claims her looks were damaged in that accident. We've recently reached a legal agreement."

"What about the baby?"

Malcolm felt his face redden. He felt considerable guilt and apprehension over the matter.

"My lawyers have negotiated custody once the child is born."

Linda's heart picked up its beat. The wretched way she had been feeling since Malcolm's engagement suddenly left her.

"You've changed, Malcolm."

"After all, Turk did save my life, my dear."

"I'll come with you." Linda could not believe she had agreed to such a foolhardy thing. But the pain of not seeing or talking to him was still raw.

"I must be a masochist," she decided, "but Bea does need help."

"Can you move the timing of the shipment up?" Linda realised that Turk O'Brien was frantic to get under way.

"Maybe to ten days from now."

Tyler told them that he would add two coffins from his own show room, put air holes in them and prepare his two trucks for the journey.

"Two coffins?"

"There might be a composite of Turk at the border, too, for all we know."

"I'll come along in one of my motorhomes," Gus Gustafson volunteered. "One of the ones used for shooting movies. That way we can cook, sleep in it and avoid restaurants and motels."

"Perfect," Tyler advised. "I'll take care of the details this afternoon and have my brokerage firm prepare the custom forms. I'll speed everything up. We can leave in ten days at the most."

Esther Goodenough advised everyone to stay away from Tyler's Funeral Home in the meantime in case they were being followed.

"Except for you Turk. You had better take cover there immediately along with Bea. That private detective may find someone who identifies you and tracks you to your house. Won't do him much good if you aren't there."

"I've put the Porsche in storage."

"What about Dogzilla" Gloria queried.

"No problem!" Tyler advised. "He can stay at the funeral home, too. Angus is already there. We'll fly them down once Turk and Bea get settled in Mexico."

"Esther and I will keep an eye on the dogs when you leave," Art Maloney volunteered.

"Virgie and I will alternate with you," Frank Simpson insisted.

Virginia Kelly nodded in agreement. "Maybe we could have some of our sessions in Tyler's place," she thought. Her son and daughter and their spouses were asking what was in the large trunk in her bedroom. "I'll ask Frank to move the trunk over there for a while."

CHAPTER 24.
False Lead.

Norm Dixon was discreetly following Gus Gustafson when he noticed him turning into one of the wealthy estates at the top of the mountain. He was convinced the movie producer was one of the people who had removed Bea Broughton from the care home. The detective was surprised to find him pulling into the large estate at the top of the mountain.

"I'll be damned. These seniors include some very wealthy and powerful people." He pulled over down the street and inserted the address into his laptop.

"Malcolm Brooks lives there. My God, the CEO of Brooks Enterprises. Don't tell me he's a member of this club."

Norm instantly realised that the large estate he was viewing was a perfect place to have hidden Bea Broughton and for that matter the mysterious fellow she had been seeing. The place was big enough to hold a small army. The detective took in the security features around Malcolm Brook's house as he pretended to be checking out a city map in case anybody took notice of him. He noted the high wall all around the estate going most of the way down the mountain. He looked at the large, coded lock on the gate.

"That would be difficult to get through," he noted. Norm detected the presence of an alarm system on the entrance door and around all the windows of the house.

"All dependent on electricity," he noted.

Norm glanced around and started as he noticed one of Malcolm's house cars moving toward the gate. The gate sprang open to the signal of a remote control and the car came closer. He stared at his map hoping they would think he was a tourist but turned his head in time to notice that the middle-aged occupants of the car going out the front gate were likely Malcolm's household servants. Right after them came Gus Gustafson's car and a well-dressed man who he presumed might be Malcolm Brooks himself.

"There's just one car left in the driveway. Expensive. Probably belongs to Malcolm Brooks. The house must be empty. This might be a chance to look inside and see if Bea Broughton is hiding there."

The large detective contemplated breaking into Malcolm Brook's residence.

"Big penalty if I get caught. Might lose my license."

He had been keeping Gus Gustafson under surveillance for some time since his suspicion that Gus was one of the dog greeting people at the care home the night Bea disappeared but this was the first time he had trailed him to Malcolm Brook's residence. He was very familiar with Gus's usual schedule and the trip up the hill had been a surprise.

"Dog walking park, eight to nine. Movie office, nine-thirty to four thirty. Stops by his favourite health club and does a workout for an hour until five thirty, and then drives himself home. Eats dinner with his wife and often they go out in the evening." '

Norm glanced at his watch. It was 10:30 in the morning.

"Perfect place for Bea Broughton to be hiding," the detective told himself again. "Bet the servants won't be back until this afternoon. I can't miss this opportunity. Might be the break I've been waiting for."

The big man put on a jogging jacket and runners, started jogging next to Malcolm Brook's fence, waited until he reached a spot where Malcolm's neighbours could not see him from the street and made a lumbering run at Malcolm's fence. As he reached the high, metal fence he desperately leaped at the fence and grabbed onto it as high up as he could. He pulled his bulk up with great difficulty and barely managed to hurl himself over the top. Norm landed with a whump and pulled himself to his feet with difficulty.

"Got to lose weight," his body told him. "Too much sitting around watching people in this job." The detective limped slowly toward the house. His right heel had still not healed from the Pitbull attack. The detective spotted a window that could not be seen from the street. He glanced at the alarm system on the window and quickly cut a key wire. A quick prodding of the window lock with the specialized tools he always carried had the window open. Norm had to wiggle frantically to get his large body through the window and he landed with a bang in Malcolm Brook's living room.

"Thank God! Doesn't seem to be anyone here."

Norm desperately tried to get his breath back as he pulled himself up from the floor. The sight of a large, boa constrictor coiled on a wooden perch inside a glass cage fired up his already activated adrenaline. The big man hastily glanced around.

"My God, what else has he got in this place?"

Norm felt his body shudder as whooping from Malcolm's Howler monkeys that he kept in a glassed in porch near the dining room reached him. He glanced at the tropical fish tank covering one wall of the living room and realised that it contained two large, oval, brown fish with large teeth.

"Pyrannas, he thought anxiously. "I wonder where the black widow spiders are."

Norm inspected the kitchen, Malcolm's office and the other rooms on the first floor. Nobody was present there or in the servant's quarters. Norm labouriously climbed the long staircase leading up to the bedroom area on the top floor.

"Bea Broughton would be there, if she's here," he thought.

He searched the upper four bedrooms but no one was there.

"Maybe the Master Bedroom," he thought hopefully. He pushed the door open and started in surprise. The room was occupied but not with the person he was expecting. A huge Sheep Dog sleeping on the bed suddenly awoke.

"My God, Malcolm Brooks is in on this. That Sheep Dog looks just like the one in John Broughton's composite."

"Nice doggy," he screamed as the large dog took one look at Norm, jumped up in surprise and started barking and growling furiously. The detective made for the door but the dog leaped at him and landed on his back before he could get out. Norm crashed to the floor with a bang. The dog lunged at his outstretched arms, barking furiously. Teeth sank in unmercifully and Norm felt himself being dragged further into the room.

The detective had frightening images of his shredded body being found later by the household servants. He managed to brace himself against the wall and landed a large kick on the huge dog's chest. The dog flew backwards and Norm scrambled for the door. An end table crashed and the lamp on it came tumbling down. The dog leaped back to his feet. Norm's large body blocked the door but he did not manage to close it in time to keep the dog in. Norm gasped as he could feel the huge Sheep Dog breath as it crashed down the stairs after him.

He made it to the bottom gasping for breath but the dog caught up to him as he reached the living room. Norm screamed as the dog leaped at his chest when he turned to face him and fell backward. The impact threw the detective into the glass Pyranna tank and to Norms's horror the glass broke under his large weight. The fish spilled out of the tank along with their water. Norm screamed as one bit him on his face as it glanced across it on its way to the floor. Norm placed his hand on the bite and blood dripped off.

Norm stared in horror as the large fish wriggled desperately in what remained of their water on the living room floor. His horror turned to relief, though, as the large Sheep Dog started lunging at the fish instead of at him.

"Now's my chance to escape," he thought. The sound of the Howler monkeys screeching in their cages echoed in his ears as he managed to reach the window through which he had entered. The dog continued to chase the fish. Norm gasped as he again pushed his body through the open window again. He wiggled out and landed heavily on the grass. He forced himself to suppress his fear and managed to stand up, shut the window and maneuvered the window lock closed again. Despite his heart pounding fiercely Norm took the time to reconnect the alarm wire.

The detective could not believe his eyes as he turned to head to the fence. The largest bird he had ever seen came charging at him across the lawn.

"My God!" he screamed as he lumbered desperately toward the fence. The bird was as big as an ostrich and as Norm looked at it his heart started pumping furiously as he noticed the sharp, razor claws on its legs. Norm reached the fence but as he leaped desperately up and grabbed onto the fence the large bird ripped at his seat with its sharp beak.

"God!" Norm screamed as he struggled to hold his grip on the fence. Fear shot adrenaline into the detective's body and he somehow managed to throw himself over the top of the fence. He landed with a heavy crash that knocked his breath out. The big man staggered to his feet and felt the back of his pants. They were wet with blood from the bird's attack. Norm lumbered down the street toward his car.

"Broughton's going to pay big bucks for this."

As he lumbered down the sidewalk closer to the house Norm could hear the cacophony of the whooping of Howler monkeys, the sheep dog's fierce barking and numerous crashes as the dog chased after the doomed Pyrannas through Malcolm Brook's living room. He finally reached his car and sighed with relief that he had made it out of the estate alive. As he calmed somewhat and investigated the damage to his body inside his car he experienced a huge feeling of disappointment that Bea Broughton had not been in the house.

"Bea Broughton wasn't there," he acknowledged his mistake. "If anyone ever figures out what really happened I'll lose my license. Maybe that would be a good thing. I need to find some other line of work. Wonder if a Pyranna bite is poisonous?"

Later that afternoon Gus Gustafson dropped Malcolm off in front of his driveway and drove off. Malcolm wondered why a glass company truck and a carpet cleaning truck were parked there. He wondered why Trump, who was out in the courtyard, slunk off behind the house instead of greeting Malcolm like he usually did. Trump seemed to have bandages on his feet and was limping rather badly. He went into his house to find his custom built Pyranna tank being repaired by a glass company employee and his living room carpet being cleaned by a carpet cleaning outfit. The living room furniture was stacked in the dining room next to the glassed in porch holding the Howler monkeys and Malcolm could see that much of his collection of art objects from around the world was chipped and cracked if not outright destroyed. Malcolm forced himself to stay calm.

"Whatever happened?" he questioned his butler who was supervising the workers. "An earthquake? And where are Vicious and Reprehensible?"

"Gone, Sir."

"Gone, you mean as in dead?"

"I'm so sorry Mr. Brooks. I found them in the dining room on the floor. It was Trump, Sir. Seems to have somehow broken the glass in the fish tank and chased the Pyrannas all over the place before they died. When the housekeeper and I were out purchasing supplies and you were having lunch with Mr. Gustafson."

"Good Lord!" Malcolm went into what was left of his bar and poured himself a whiskey. "Talk about the impermanence of everything in this life. Honey Pratt is right."

"Is Trump all right?"

"Dr. Daniels came over and took care of him, Sir? She said he'll be all right. Just to keep him quiet for a few days until the cuts on his paws and the bites from the Pyrannas heal."

"Linda came?"

"Yes, Sir. The other veterinarian that's taking care of your animals was busy at an emergency so he contacted her. She came right over, took care of Trump, gave the Howler monkeys a sedative that calmed them down, sympathized about the loss of the Pyrannas and told me to tell you that she would be back to remove the dog's stitches in several days."

Malcolm went into his bedroom, noted that Trump had done a number in there as well as he looked at crashed furniture, broken lamp and piles of sheep hair. Malcolm sat down heavily in an armchair and gulped down his whiskey.

"Linda was here and I didn't get a chance to talk to her." Malcolm winced in surprise as he realised he was more concerned about missing Linda than his dead Pyrannas and destroyed large art collection.

CHAPTER 25.
The Journey.

Esther Goodenough's mind was not on her task as she pulled into Tyler Thompson's show room and parked her luxury Mazda sports car. She pulled out Tyler's key to his residence from her pocket and continued on automatic pilot to go pick up Dogzilla and Angus. She managed to pick up the chest from the trunk of the car that Virginia Kelly had asked her to bring to Tyler's residence. Esther allowed herself a stab of jealousy as she thought about the contents of the chest.

"They should be well on their way down the freeway," Esther glanced at her watch. She had been told via her a cell phone call from Tyler Thompson that all three vehicles in the convoy to Mexico were leaving several hours before. Esther's mind, however, was on her latest lunch and deep talk with Art Thompson. Esther had been hopefully waiting for Art to move past the chaste kisses he was giving her.

Her heart experienced a combination of warmth and then deep disappointment as Art had finally confided that he thought a lot of her but that he had a medical condition that no longer allowed him sexual intimacy. The information had been such a shock to Esther. Their lively conversations and lunches almost every day since Pegasus had unceremoniously dumped her into the rock and barnacled sand at the dog park had somehow awakened what she had thought were long dead feelings of sexuality. Esther had been hoping for quite some time that Art was going to move past the warm and intimate kisses that they had been sharing.

"It's too late for me to pull back now," Esther gave a short laugh. Her habitual sense of humour was kicking in. "I absolutely adore the man."

Esther smiled as she stared at the trunk and recalled the joy that Virgie seemed to be getting out of her very hot connection to Frank Simpson.

"Makes me blush," Esther thought jealously as she imagined the vivid picture Virgie was painting when she confided her rather extreme sexual encounters with Frank.

"Perhaps it's a good thing," Esther concluded. "I'm not sure my body at this age could stand up to the things they are doing to themselves." Her sense of humour really kicked in as she continued to think about Virgie and Frank. Esther imagined Virgie's son or daughter discovering her and Frank's secret treasure chest of toys and costumes.

"We'll be having to save Virgie from the Down Memory Lane Care Home too," Esther thought, knowing the narrow mindedness of Virgie's religiously groomed children.

She opened the door and laughed as Dogzilla bolted down the stairs as soon as he saw Pegasus. Little Angus rushed up to her and looked extremely disappointed when he discovered she was not his owner, Bea. He whined and she picked the little dog up in her arms.

"Won't be long," she assured him.

Esther deposited Virgie's trunk in one of Tyler Thompson's bedroom as Virgie had requested.

"I wonder what Tyler's housekeeper will think if she looks inside that," she laughed. "Good thing they keep a lock on it."

Esther vacated Tyler's residence, gathered up the dogs and

started up her luxury Mazda. She headed off to the dog park largely on automatic pilot. She made her decision as she moved into the parking lot.

"Art and I have such a lovely connection. We can talk to each other about anything and it would be lovely to do some travelling with the man."

Esther decided that sex at her age was not all it was cracked up to be anyway. She planted a huge kiss and hug on the uptight stockbroker as he came out of his car to greet her. He broke into a beaming smile and hugged her solidly in return.

"Maybe Viagra would help," Esther thought as Art's closeness aroused again what she had thought were long dead sexual longings. "If not, I'll just have the world's greatest friendship. Arthur's even showing me how to evaluate my stocks on his laptop. This is a win-win situation."

Dogzilla and Pegasus leaped out of the car as Art opened the door. They fell in with Mozart, the Blue Healer, who was waiting for them on the walkway and all three dogs moved beside each other shoulder to shoulder and galloped toward the ocean. Art and Esther followed with Art carrying Angus in his arms. Norm Dixon, watching in his car at the back of the parking lot freaked out.

"Christ, that's Bea Broughton's dog and the mystery Rottweiler."

Norm's mind flew into elation at the break in his case. He had all but given up hope that Bea Broughton was alive. He was hugely ashamed of the mess he must have caused at Malcolm Brook's residence.

"All I have to do is follow them back to where the dogs are being kept. Their owners are sure to be there as well."

Two hours later the detective watched as Dogzilla and Angus were returned to Tyler's residence by Art Maloney.

"Hell, the Funeral Home, I should have known." Norm cursed himself for not suspecting the location sooner. He had followed dog walking club members to the Funeral Home several times but had concluded they were just meeting with Tyler Thompson. He waited till Art Maloney headed off and then went into the Funeral Show Room to track down the dogs and their owners.

"Those dogs?" he enquired as a young man came to greet him. "The ones that came in with that fellow a few moments ago?"

"What's it to you?" the employee demanded.

Norm pulled out his Private Detective identification.

"Want to talk to their owners!" he explained.

"Not possible," the young salesman told him. "You'll have to talk to the fellow that brought the dogs in if you want to know something about them. Don't know when he'll be back."

"Where's your boss? I'll speak to him."

"Good luck. He's off to Mexico for several weeks."

Norm Dixon's heart stopped.

"Mexico?"

Norm's intuition kicked into play as the salesclerk told him that his boss had just gone off with a shipment of coffins to Mexico that very morning.

He managed to get the salesperson to reveal the destination of the coffins and the route down.

"Guadalajara, he's going down the freeway and across at the Nogales border crossing, that's all I know."

Norm realised he had to act fast. He went out to his car and headed for the freeway. He picked up his cell phone on the way and made a call.

"Got a strong lead," he told John Broughton. "Good

chance your mother is alive and headed for Mexico. Can I count on you to fund whatever is needed to track her down?"

He waited as he could hear John Broughton tell his wife the latest developments.

"Tell the detective we want him to locate your mother and bring her back to the care home even if he has to do it against her will," Orphelia instructed.

"They know she doesn't want to come back," the detective noted. His anxiety about what he was doing started up again. He started as Orphelia's voice came over the phone.

"There's big bucks in it for you if you bring the woman back to the care home," John Broughton's wife advised.

The large detective had a moment of conscience.

"What if I have to break the law?"

"On hundred thousand for starters," the woman ordered.

"And the expenses?"

"Of course."

The detective suppressed his misgivings.

"I need to go into something else," he rationalized as he hung up the phone. "That money will give me a new start."

Many miles away two large trucks and a motorhome made their way down the freeway toward Mexico making sure to leave enough space for anyone wanting to pass to manoeuvre through them. Tyler Thompson led the way. Honey Pratt and Bourbon were seated next to him while Bea Broughton, Turk O'Brien and Inferno rested in what looked like a large, dog bed complete with pillows in the back of the truck between the coffins. Every time the large truck made a stop Bea and Turk had been told to be alert for sounds of the padlock securing the back door opening, in which case they were to climb into the specially prepared coffins and bring the tops down on themselves.

"We're on our way at last," Turk gave Bea a huge hug as he noted the sadness on her face. "You're thinking of your grandchildren, aren't you?"

"I'll call them as soon as we're in Mexico."

"Of course."

"Maybe John will reconsider."

Turk laughed. "He won't have much of a choice when Malcolm's lawyers get through with him."

Turk looked around the inside of the utilitarian, cargo truck.

"Not the way I wanted to take you on a vacation," Turk apologised.

"I'm so grateful to you and the others," Bea replied.

In the cab in front Tyler and Honey were having a heart-to-heart conversation.

"How's Charlotte taking your going to Mexico?" Tyler drew Honey closer to him and rested one of his arms around her shoulders.

"Not well! I had to tell her I was going with you."

Honey recounted the argument that had occurred when she had told her daughter of the journey. She told Tyler that Charlotte had begged her to see a psychiatrist about her unfulfilled father or authority figure complex. Tyler laughed.

"You're not very daughterly," he complained.

"I know." Honey moved closer to Tyler until he warned her that he needed room to manoeuvre the large truck.

"Later," he promised.

As Honey sighed and allowed him enough space to manoeuvre the truck Tyler marvelled in his mind at the woman he had met so late in life.

"She's everything I've ever wanted," he acknowledged.

Tyler added up all her good qualities. A great sense

of humour was at the top of the list, followed by spirited, attractive, philosophical, responsible, empathetic, good natured, intelligent, fun to be with, and sexually responsive.

"I should have met her years ago," he thought wistfully. "Maybe I would have even had the family I've always wanted."

"Do you think Charlotte would ever accept me as a stepfather?" he blurted out loud.

Tyler laughed as Honey nearly jumped up from the seat in surprise.

"You're missing a step here, Sugar!"

"Just a rhetorical question!" Tyler smiled as Honey looked immensely relieved.

"That Girl? She's rather stepfather challenged, y'all should know. Never did trust my last two suitors, but come to think of it neither did I."

Directly behind Tyler's truck, Malcolm Brooks, Trump and Linda were sitting in that order in the front seat of the second cargo truck. Cleo was in the back of the truck. Every time Malcolm was forced to engage the clutch to shift gears he started to breathe rather heavily as his right lower leg was still in a cast and the movement caused him some pain.

Linda was sitting quietly next to the passengers' window glad that Trump was sitting in between herself and Malcolm. She had no desire to engage in a conversation about his life. She had decided that Malcolm was probably just looking for the next thirty something year old to become involved with, if indeed he did not already have one lined up to be a mother for Monica's child when it was born. Linda was suddenly very weary of her long years of unrequited love and had no wish to experience another disillusionment. However, her wish for silence was quickly ended.

"Trade places with Trump, will you Linda and open the window, he needs some air," Malcolm ordered.

Linda opened the window a hair and switched places with the dog. The large Sheep Dog placed his head at the top next to the opening, gasping loudly. Linda relented and put the window down further. A blast of cold air struck her and she zipped up the sweater she was wearing. Trump put his whole head out the window and panted as he savoured every exotic smell he inhaled. Linda ignored his barking and thrashing as he smelled and then visually sighted his first herd of cattle in a field near the highway.

"This is going to be a long trip," Linda sighed to herself. She wondered how her own dog Cleo was making out in the back of the truck. Malcolm sighed again as he shifted gears several times on a long hill.

"You should switch places with Gus," Linda advised. "The motorhome has an automatic transmission."

"Only if you come with me," Malcolm laughed. "I'm not going to be trapped in a three-bed motorhome with Gloria all the way to Mexico."

The absurdity of the situation struck Linda as funny. Here she was sitting next to Malcolm with a still not completely dead desire to get closer to him while Malcolm appeared oblivious to her intent. Meanwhile he was avoiding Gloria who was apparently oblivious to the fact that Malcolm did not want closeness with her.

"It's like Shakespeare. Midsummer night's Dream." She burst out in a full, roaring laugh, thinking of Gloria's wager.

"What's so funny?"

Linda didn't want to tell him. She switched to another topic.

"You know that Gus and Gloria have an open marriage?"

"Only too well. Gloria has told me about that at least ten times over the years."

"Why do you suppose they do that?"

Linda was shocked as Malcolm told her about Gus and Gloria's relationship. He told her that neither Gloria nor Gus was ever into commitment. That when she and Gus met Gloria had at least six handsome leading men chasing after her and Gus had all his leading ladies chasing after him.

"So?"

"You know the statistics about Hollywood marriages? Most of them end in divorce after anywhere from one day to three years."

"I still don't get it."

Malcolm told Linda that Gus and Gloria had a heart to heart talk when they realised they were in love with each other. Gus told her that the only way a marriage could possibly last for them was to make it an open marriage. That when they found themselves seriously attracted to another they would have the right to have a fling with no questions asked.

"It seems to have worked for them."

"Right. Much better than my own marriage. It only made it through ten years."

"You still miss your ex-wife, don't you Malcolm?"

Malcolm gave out a startle reaction.

"Don't be ridiculous. Why do you say that?"

Linda told him about him calling his wife's name in the ambulance on the way to the hospital the first time.

"I did that? Must have been having a nightmare."

Linda realised he was trying to laugh the incident off rather than confront his past. She told him that it was better to forgive and forget and that sometimes people required a therapist to help them do just that.

"I did that a long time ago, my dear."

Malcolm did not believe his words for a minute. The

revelation that he had spoken Blanche's name aloud in the ambulance had shaken him much more than he had admitted. He did not tell Linda but Every time he got intimate with one of his youthful girlfriends he imagined he was making love to his former wife. She had been close to their age when she had gone off with one of his business rivals.

"Maybe Linda is right?" Malcolm found himself questioning. "Maybe I

should make an effort to try and deal with my past."

In the motorhome behind Malcolm, Gus grew more and more irritated as he was forced to step on the brake yet again as the truck in front of him slowed and hesitated more than it should have.

"Malcolm's having trouble shifting," Gus said to Gloria who was in the passenger side. He picked up the walkie talkie from the dashboard and called Tyler's phone.

"Hollywood 1 to Inferno. Come in Inferno."

"Inferno here." Gus smiled as Tyler's voice came over the phone.

"Find a safe place to pull over," Gus requested. "I need to change places with Malcolm. He's having trouble shifting."

"Right Hollywood 1."

Twenty minutes later Tyler pulled into a rest spot on the highway and waited until both Malcolm and Gus pulled their rigs up next to him.

The ladies and Tyler Thompson all went in the direction of the rest room but Malcolm and Gus remained at the picnic table.

At the picnic table Gus told Malcolm that he needed to switch vehicles.

"Can see you're having trouble with the clutch."

Malcolm told Gus that he would appreciate switching

but that he had to take Gloria with him into the front of the truck.

"Why?"

Malcolm decided that he didn't want to tell his best friend that he was afraid that his wife would hit on him.

"I brought Linda along to take care of Trump. She needs to be with me and him. His feet are still not quite healed from that encounter with my Pyranna tank."

"Hell, is that all you brought her for? Look, if you're not interested in Linda why don't you give me a chance?"

Malcolm was shocked at Gus's suggestion.

"Linda is too nice a woman to be just a short-term affair," he protested.

"Suddenly you're protective of Linda? Butt out! You've had more than a chance at her. I want a turn."

"That's what happened with Blanche," Malcolm suddenly felt himself turning white with anger.

"You Son of A Bitch! You turned Blanche on when I was too occupied with business and then when you dropped her she went off with one of my business rivals."

"I thought we settled all that years ago," Gus protested. "And look at all the lovelies I've sent your way over the years in reparations."

Malcolm's anger suddenly left him as fast as it had hit. He thought of him and Gus's long friendship.

"I'm sorry. I don't know what came over me."

"Face it Malcolm. You're jealous of my interest in Linda."

"Maybe I am?" Malcolm tried to make sense of his sudden anger flare. A huge mixture of emotions was upsetting his usual calm.

"Look Malcolm," Gus told him. "Because of our friendship I'll give you a while to think this out. But only until the middle of the next state. I'm telling you. I'm really interested in Linda."

Gloria and Linda interrupted the conversation as they returned. They were startled to find the two men in deep conversation.

"What's up?" Gloria demanded.

"We're trading places with Malcolm and Linda."

Gus got up from the table and handed the motorhome keys to Malcolm. Malcolm gave the keys to the truck to Gus. He limped over to the motor home. Linda rounded up Trump and Cleo and followed. Gus, Gloria, Honey and Tyler gathered up their dogs and went over to their remaining vehicles and got in.

As they sat down in the second cargo truck and Gus started up the motor to follow Tyler out, he thought of Malcolm and placed his hand on his forehead.

"Malcolm is a dolt," he said to his wife of many years.

"What's he done now?"

"It's what he hasn't done. That moron doesn't seem to know that Linda is crazy about him. Has been for years, apparently."

"He doesn't appreciate us older women. Can't get beyond the attraction of young things, apparently."

Gus shook his head.

"I don't think so. If you ask me, it's more likely that Malcolm is afraid of older ladies that possess both the looks and intelligence of his ex-wife."

"That's very perceptive of you Darling. Thanks for giving us older ladies credit."

"You deserve it, believe me."

"You could be right. Malcolm's dates all these years have certainly not been rocket scientists."

Gus told Gloria that it took a lot of self esteem to date someone as attractive and intelligent as Linda. That he figured Malcolm had never got over his wife Blanche leaving him and that he bet Malcolm had some kind of inferiority complex that he could not shake. Probably about his prowess in bed.

Gloria whistled.

"My God. I never suspected that. The man is handsome enough and his wealth certainly would act as an aphrodisiac of some sort."

"I'm going to come on strong to Linda and see if I can get Malcolm jealous enough to do something about it? You don't mind, do you?"

Gloria looked at her husband oddly.

"Anything I can do to help?"

"Come on to Malcolm. Maybe you could give him some confidence that an attractive, intelligent, older woman would actually appreciate him."

Gloria laughed. She did not want to tell her husband that she had been doing exactly that for years.

"Gus's conclusions must be wrong," she thought. "Actually I think Malcolm's just into revenge. Showing off with all the young things to goad his ex-wife."

"All right Dear, if you insist."

By nightfall the three vehicles had reached the border of the first state. Tyler drove into a RV park just before the state border and shut off his motor. Gus parked into another spot and left room for the motorhome in the centre. He went to pay the camping fee before the owner realised the number of dogs present in the vehicles. The rest of the crew with the exception of Bea and Turk moved into the motorhome. Bea and Turk had been instructed to stay put no matter what.

Turk groaned as he reached into the hidden food supply

and pulled out cereal bars, potato chips, and canned vegetable juice.

Bea comforted him.

"Don't worry. We'll make up for it in Mexico."

"Could have left some ale," Turk complained?

Back in the motor home, Linda, Honey and Gloria started heating up food in the kitchen. In a few minutes they could hear the joyous barks of the dogs as Gus, Malcolm and Tyler let them all out for a run near the river. By the time the food was ready the men had finished walking the dogs and returned. Gus secured Bourbon to the back door of Tyler's truck and Cleo to the back door of the truck he was driving. He brought the other dogs over to the picnic table by the motorhome and doled out their evening dinner from a large bag of dry pet food. He made sure that Cleo and Bourbon had their share as well as a large bowl of fresh water.

Conversation was limited inside the motorhome as all were weary from their long drive. Gus decided to assign the beds.

"It's an early start tomorrow," he encouraged the others to hit the hay. "Gloria and I will take the back bedroom with Gigi and Inuvik, Tyler, you and Honey will have to climb up on the bed over the cab and Malcolm, this table folds down into a double bed. Trump and Inferno can go in the back of the trucks."

"What about Bea and Turk? I'll take some food over for them."

"No," Tyler ordered. "I've left a supply of dry food and liquids in a hidden place in their truck. We can't take the chance of raising suspicions."

Shortly afterward Linda found herself in bed with Malcolm. They were even physically touching each other as the bed was quite small. She laughed to herself as a slight snore alerted her that he had fallen asleep the moment his head had hit the pillow.

"I must be daft," Linda mused as she realised that she had been hoping for just such a situation as this for the last ten years. To make things even worse a slight rocking of the van told Linda that Honey and Tyler were making love in the bed above the driver's seat. Minutes later Linda clenched her teeth as she realised she was becoming physically aroused. The feeling became quite intense.

"It's Malcolm's physical presence so close," she mused. "Now what am I supposed to do. Wake everyone up as I take a cold shower?"

Linda tried shifting positions, removing covers, scrunching herself into the wall below the window, thinking of anything but Malcolm, reviewing her childhood, counting to ten thousand, revisiting her mother's funeral in her mind,

but nothing stopped the tormenting sexual arousal that was striking her.

Outside Tyler's truck, from the picnic table of an adjoining campsite, Norm Dixon was eying the Pitbull tied to the back door of one of the trucks. The detective had broken every speeding law in the book and had managed to catch up to Tyler's Thomson's convoy just before they had pulled into the RV campsite.

The dog seemed to be aware of his presence. It was facing him chewing one of its red phosphorescent balls.

"All I've got is intuition," Norm warned himself. "But I'm willing to bet Bea Broughton is in one of those trucks. It's best if I grab her before we reach Mexico. It would be far less complicated to take her back from this side of the border to that care home and pick up my money. I'm going to have to get inside those trucks and find out."

"Maybe the dog doesn't remember me," Norm thought hopefully. "But I'll try the other truck first. He got up and moved slowly over to the other truck beside the motorhome. Cleo gave out a sharp, warning bark. Norm retreated and moved toward the first truck. Bourbon did not bark but his eyes followed the large detective's every move.

"I've got to stop being afraid. The dog is quiet now but he'll react if he senses my fear."

Norm cautiously approached Bourbon. The dog still did not seem to be reacting, just chewing its red ball. The detective took a deep breath and decided to push his luck. He slowly moved further toward Tyler's truck and spotted the padlock on the back of the door. He reached for his bolt cutters. Bourbon waited until the detective was within his range and was reaching for the lock. He spit his ball out of his mouth and grabbed the detective by his right foot. His teeth sank through the leather of the detective's shoe and he bit deep into the foot. It was the same foot he had chewed on before. Norm muffled a scream as he could feel the stitches which still had not healed pulling out.

Norm desperately tried shaking the dog loose with his leg. Bourbon hung on tight. Blood was now pouring out of Norm's shoe. Norm kicked the dog as hard as he could with his other foot. The Pit Bull held on even more tightly. Norm desperately tried to pull his foot out of his shoe. There was a flesh ripping sound. Intense pain seared through Norm Dixon's mind and his foot suddenly came free from the shoe. Norm was sent sprawling on to the concrete pad with a thud. Fear helped Norm pull himself up and he turned to make it back to his car. However Bourbon spit out the shoe, and grabbed the seat of Norm's pants before he could get out of his range.

"Christ," Norm smothered a scream as the Pitbull sank

his teeth into the flesh of his seat. He could feel the stitches from the attack of the large bird at Malcolm Brook's yard pulling out.

"Oh no," Norm realised as he managed to pull his seat free but felt his flesh rip out in the grip of the dog's teeth in the process. Bourbon's jaws were firmly locked on the cloth of his pants and boxer shorts. The dog pulled him down to the road. In deepening desperation Norm reached for his belt and unzipped his zipper. His pants and Boxer shorts were pulled down in a flash. The now, a half-naked detective leaped clear as the Pitbull was hanging on for dear life to the pants. The bleeding detective realised he was going to have to sacrifice his pants. He placed his hands on his genitals to protect them from the dog, moved away from the truck and frantically lumbered towards his car as fast as his bulk, and his damaged bleeding foot plus rear end would allow.

Cleo was not as quiet as Bourbon when he saw the detective moving toward his car in a running limp. She let out another sharp bark as the detective passed her truck. Norm placed his jacket around his naked and bleeding lower half, threw himself into his car as he reached it, ignored the burning pain from the dog bites, turned on the engine, reversed and headed out of the campground.

"I should have brought some fresh meat to distract the dogs," the detective cursed. " Damn, I'll have to go get some as well as shorts, pants, a first aid kit and some shoes. It's the only way those dogs will let me close."

"Where the Hell am I going to find meat, pants, Boxer shorts and a first aid kit at 12:00 at night?" Norm realised through sharp burning pain and the frantic thumping of his heart that he was going to have to find some pain killers and something to calm his nerves as well.

Linda heard Cleo's barks through the haze of sensuality that was striking her. She realised that Cleo only gave that kind of bark when an intruder was present.

"I better take a look," she realised. Linda moved carefully over Malcolm ignoring her instinctual urges to fling herself on him and managed to get to the floor without disturbing him. As she quietly opened the motorhome door, Linda spotted the headlights of Norm Dixon's car leaving the RV park.

"That's odd," she thought. Linda quietly crept out the motorhome door and went over to Cleo. The dog panted rapidly and she gratefully licked Linda's face. She barked and looked anxiously over at the campsite next to the truck. Linda could see the embers of a fire in the campsite fire pit.

"What's going on?" Gus's voice suddenly startled Linda. He loomed up beside her dressed in his robe and pajamas.

"I heard Cleo bark and came to investigate."

"There's a fire in that campsite next to us."

"Right, I saw the lights of a vehicle leaving when I opened the motorhome door."

Gus looked toward the second truck.

"What's Bourbon doing? Looks like he's got something he's shaking around."

Linda and Gus walked over to Bourbon.

"I'll get that out of his mouth."

Linda walked up to the thrashing pit bull. She gave him a massage on his back and patted him until he managed to calm down. She worked her hands around his mouth and tugged on the object. Bourbon opened his jaws suddenly and the object sprang loose. Bourbon whined.

"What's that he's chewing?"

Gus put his flashlight on the object.

"Someone's pants and boxer shorts!" he said in absolute astonishment. "They've even got their belt attached."

Then the light caught Norm Dixon's shoe. Gus picked up the items ignoring Bourbon's pleas for him to give them back.

"Pants, boxer shorts and a shoe." Gus reached into the pockets but nothing was in them.

Gus's fingers felt something wet. He placed the light on the objects.

"Blood! God, someone must have been trying to get into the truck and Bourbon chewed them up."

"We had better get out of here right now," Gus decided. He went back to the motorhome and Linda could hear him rousing everyone to get up. She took Bourbon into the front of one of the trucks, praised him for chasing off the intruder and then went back to the motorhome to dress herself.

Within ten minutes Gus had the two trucks and the motorhome back on the freeway and approaching the state border. He was now leading the way in Tyler's truck and as they passed the state line he headed off the freeway toward the Coastal route, slowing slightly to make sure that Tyler and Malcolm had followed.

"Whoever that was won't think we switched highways," he said confidently to Gloria next to him in the cargo truck.

In the motorhome Linda was having a battle with herself. Despite what had happened she realised that Malcolm's physical presence so close was still sexually turning her on. One part of her mind wanted to finally confide to Malcolm that she was attracted to him. Another was telling her that she was going to make a complete fool of herself if she did. Instead she told Malcolm what had happened outside.

"Whoever that was must be half naked and bleeding," she ended with a laugh. Malcolm joined in the laughter but then changed the subject.

"We've got to stop sleeping together in that small bed," Malcolm confided. Linda's mouth fell open in shock.

"My sentiments exactly!" she replied.

"I need to raise my lower leg higher. I can't even get a pillow in between you and me."

"Wait till the others fall asleep, I'll move onto the floor." Linda's hopes shattered.

"Next time we stop for gas, I'll pick up an air mattress for you."

"Thanks."

"You were uncomfortable, too?"

"Yes, too cramped," Linda lied, glad that she had not revealed her true feelings.

Back in Tyler's truck Turk O'Brien and Bea were wondering what was going on. Turk moved forward and knocked on the window between the cab of the truck. Honey Pratt shoved it open.

"What's going on?"

"Cleo woke Linda up. Seems there was someone trying to get into your truck. Bourbon must have stopped him. Chewed him up quite a bit by the look of it. Left his pants when the dog wouldn't let go I imagine and his shoe. Linda saw the car lights when whoever it was left the campsite."

"Maybe that detective?"

"Likely."

"Damn!"

Tyler broke in to say that Gus had shifted them all to the coastal route to throw the fellow off if he came back.

"Can you stop at the next town? I want to pick up a gun."

"No way, Turk," Tyler warned. "You can't take those things across the border."

"At least stop and get us a couple of coffees."

In his mind Turk decided to secretly try and get hold of a weapon any time they stopped.

Honey Pratt nodded. "Sure, Sugar, it must be like a sensory deprivation tank in there."

Three hours later Norm Dixon's heart nearly stopped as he drove back into the RV campsite only to discover his fugitives gone. He roared around and moved back onto the freeway with a vengeance.

"Good thing this is a powerful car," he thought. And that all night general store and gas station sold pants, boxer shorts, shoes, meat and a first aid kit. Norm stepped on the gas and quickly reached thirty miles per hour past the speed limit. He tried to ignore the irregular thumping of his heart and the pain in his seat and foot. He realised that he was thoroughly traumatized at the ordeal he had gone through.

"Can't be any cops on duty this time of the night," he said to himself. "A good thing that general store guy didn't question me about what happened to my pants and shoe? Believed me that some dog had attacked me for no reason. A good thing I had my wallet in my jacket pocket. And the jacket to cover my chewed up ass. Hope I don't get some god awful disease from those bites." Norm bit his lip to ignore the pain as his bandaged foot was still throbbing and his disinfected, bandaged seat was still burning from Bourbon's attack.

By dawn the frantic detective admitted to himself that either the rigs had pulled off somewhere again or they were not on the freeway.

"I'll need a plane to find them," he realised. He pulled over to the side of the freeway and took a look at a map of the state. He was an hour from a major airport.

"Surely there's a pilot and plane I can rent. I've got to get possession of that woman before they go over the border."

By noon he had covered the entire freeway to the California state line and all of the RV sites within ten miles of it. Norm was oblivious to the serenity and wild beauty of the area.

"They must have switched highways," he concluded. The pilot landed at a small field to refuel again and Norm directed him to fly to the Coastal Route. By three o'clock he was half way through Oregon on the Coastal Route when he spotted the convoy.

"That's them," he yelled to the pilot. "Where's the nearest landing spot with a rental car agency?"

The pilot told him it would be about twenty minutes flying time. Norm motioned him to go for it.

"Newport," Norm looked at the map. "They are near Newport. I bet they pull off before dark. They'll be three-quarters through Oregon." Norm reached for his package of fresh steak.

"Those dogs ain't going to turn away from this," he thought confidently.

CHAPTER 26.
Second Stage.

By dusk Gus figured out that he had better find somewhere to stop for a while. He was starting to go to sleep at the wheel. The landscape was getting hard to see.

"I'd better take the next well-lit, RV sign, Darling," he told Gloria.

"Edgar's Roost, " Gloria shouted several minutes later. Gus pulled off the highway onto a narrow road and slowed to make sure Tyler and Malcolm had followed. The phone on the dashboard rang. Gus picked it up.

"Inferno to Hollywood 1."

"Hello Inferno,"

"Don't go into the RV spot," Tyler warned. "Whoever that was they would expect us to be in one."

"Roger Inferno." Gus passed Edgar's Roost. He drove on for another half an hour and then spotted a white church with a fairly large parking lot. Gus pulled in and parked around the rear of the church. The others parked beside him. They were not visible from the road.

By dawn an increasingly anxious Norm Dixon had checked out every RV access off the southern and middle sections of the Coastal Route of Oregon. The package of meat in the passenger seat had started to smell.

"I'll have to go back to the air," he sighed. "Hope

Broughton has enough money to pay for this." Norm pulled over and checked out his map again. He headed for the closest airport that looked big enough to have a plane rental.

Gus stepped out of his bedroom and nearly stepped on a slumbering Linda Daniels in the aisle of his motorhome.

"My God, Malcolm's still not sleeping with Linda," Gus shook his head in disbelief. "Newport," he said to himself. "Three quarters of the way through Oregon. He glanced at Malcolm Brooks, snoring slightly on the bed. " Malcolm, I'm going to go for it."

By the time Gus had checked on the dogs and given them a run in the churchyard Gloria and Linda had breakfast cooked. Gus ordered everyone to take their food with them and get back on the road.

"We seem to have been lucky," he told them "but I'm not taking any chances. Going to head back over to the freeway now."

"If that fellow is still following you're going to drive him nuts," Tyler laughed.

By three p.m. Norm Dixon had flown all the way down to the Mexican border. He was now thoroughly exhausted and depressed as there had been no sign of the motorhome and the cargo trucks on the Coastal Highway.

"They've vanished into thin air," he cursed. "And I've run up a small fortune in plane and pilot rentals." The package of fresh meat he was carrying with him was now smelling pungently. The detective felt desperation taking over his mind. He forced it to be still.

"The freeway," he sighed as he realised the convoy must have headed back onto it. "I'll land for the night, charter the pilot for the next morning and find a doctor to take care of my seat and foot before I develop gangrene." The large detective was feeling awful.

He told the pilot to land at the nearest airstrip and chartered him for the next day. Desperation forced him to think out a contingency plan if he was not able to locate them on the freeway the next day. His desperate mind worked out a possible solution to the problem.

"They have to come to the border sometime the next day after tomorrow or the one after," he realised. "That worker in the funeral home said that his boss always uses the Nogales border crossing. They'll likely stop for gas and Mexican car insurance at a station and Mexican insurance sales before they go across. All I have to do is watch for them just before the border. I can contact the American Border guards if I have to. They'll cooperate if I can assure them two fugitives are hiding in those trucks. But I have to be sure."

Later in San Francisco, Gus pulled into a large Walmart parking lot for the night. Tyler and Malcolm pulled in beside him.

"Walmart lets you stay for free in their parking lot," Gus explained as the others parked beside him and trudged into the motor home complete with their dogs. Even the dogs seemed tired. They slumped obediently on the floor.

"That fellow will never think of finding us in a Walmart." Tyler laughed. "How about we let Bea and Turk out of that tin can for a while."

"Good idea," Malcolm seconded.

"There's a dining room across the street," Honey Pratt pointed out the widow. "How's about we'all go and have a decent meal for a change?"

Tyler nodded enthusiastically and Gus gave a weary OK.

"We'll bring back some burgers for the dogs."

Bea and Turk blinked their eyes as they looked furtively around the large Walmart. The sunlight coming through the windows was in sharp contrast to the semi-darkness of the cargo truck.

"I have to act fast," Turk told Bea as he searched for the hunting and fishing section of Walmart. "They're expecting us at the restaurant across the street. He located the gun section and quickly purchased a hand gun. The he and Bea hid the weapon in Turk's coffin inside the large truck. They both ran across the street to the restaurant. Turk's mind was on the man pursuing them.

"Got a funny feeling that fellow hasn't given up!" Turk warned his friends as they all ordered steaks, drinks and desert. Bea ordered a Lava Flow.

"Think the switch back and forth between the highways threw him off," Gus replied.

"For how long?"

"We'll do it again. In the morning. I'll switch back to the coastal route for the run into Los Angeles."

Gus told the group that they would stay in Los Angeles for the next night and then head to the border through San Diego and Tucson. Tyler told them that the border at Nogales would require them to get automobile permits for one hundred eighty days and that they would be stopped a second time at the Federal Inspection Point, about twelve miles into Mexico, where the permits and baggage would likely be inspected. He told them they would have to pick up Mexican automobile insurance before they went over the border.

"We'll stop at one of the RV camps for the night and then get the insurance, gas and head into Mexico in the morning," Gus decided.

Gus had made certain that he sat next to Linda. Malcolm watched with growing concern as Gus engaged Linda in private conversation. He was paying much too much attention to her and Gloria was taking the opportunity to chat with him. Malcolm was finding it difficult to follow Gloria's conversation and monitor Gus's interaction with Linda at the same time. When Gus asked Linda to dance and she agreed Malcolm felt himself growing more and more apprehensive. Tyler and Honey took the opportunity to dance as well and Malcolm was left with a chatty Gloria, Bea Broughton and a visibly worried Turk O'Brien.

"I'll join you in the motorhome tomorrow," Gloria informed him. His worst fears had been confirmed. "Gus says he wants to have a long talk with Linda. About the dogs."

"Uh, thanks but I need Linda to keep an eye on Trump. He's still pretty restless and I don't want him interfering with my driving."

"Trump can join her in the truck with Gus," Gloria replied as if the switch was a done deal. Malcolm realised he had to do something drastic or Linda was going to be propositioned by Gus and Gloria was going to hit on him. The thought sent him into a fury.

"Linda can take care of herself," Malcolm tried to reason through his anger. "But look what happened to Blanche," some part of his mind warned him.

"That was thirty years ago," another part shot back.

Gloria got up to dance with Turk and Malcolm was left alone with Bea Broughton. His thoughts about Linda and Gus continued to whirl through his head. He had difficulty thinking about anything to talk to Bea about. He was too busy staring at Linda and Gus on the dance floor. They seemed to be having a great time. When the band switched into a Tango and Gus aggressively manoevered Linda through some very sexy moves Malcolm felt himself losing complete control of his emotions.

"Too bad about your engagement ending, Malcolm."

Malcolm stared at Bea.

"It's for the best," he reassured her. "Monica and I are not suited at all. She loathes animals and I like to have them constantly around."

"I understand. Your ex-wife Blanche felt the same way as Monica, you know. She simply didn't understand why you had to have all those pets. That's why she left you."

"That's why Blanche left me?" Malcolm couldn't believe his ears.

He had always assumed that it was because he was an inadequate lover. And that she had discovered that fact when Gus managed to seduce her.

"Yes. Didn't she ever tell you that she was allergic to fur and animal dander?"

Malcolm gasped. Bea was blowing his mind. He was suddenly thrown back to memories from thirty years ago. When he searched his memory, he recalled Blanche complaining time and time again that his pets were causing her asthma attacks. Malcolm realised that he had not paid any attention to his former wife's objections to his animal collection. Malcolm realised he was having a long overdue flash of insight into the reason behind his wife leaving him.

"My God," he confessed to Bea. "I just kept telling her to get allergy shots. I guess I'm not a very good listener."

"Oh well, that's all water under the bridge," Bea sighed as Turk and the others came back to the table.

By the time everyone reached the motorhome and Bea and Turk had returned to Tyler's cargo van, Malcolm was overcome with a strange mixture of emotions. His mind was spinning.

"Bea must be wrong. A wife wouldn't leave just because of your animals. No, it was because of Gus."

Fury took over Malcolm's mind.

"I'm not going to let what happened to Blanche happen to Linda," he vowed. "I guess Bea is partly right. I never listened to Blanche's concerns about my animals and she got even by taking Gus as a lover."

"My God. I wonder what Linda has been trying to tell me and I haven't been listening." Malcolm forced his memory to recall his interactions with Linda over the years. He recalled the way she looked into his eyes when they were having deep conversations and the small gifts she had always left on Christmas and his birthday. Insight finally struck Malcolm as he realised that Linda must have had a crush on him for many years.

"She's been trying to tell me but I haven't been listening."

Malcolm went over to the sink in the galley of the motorhome, pulled out a small blue pill, gulped it down with a drink of water, waited until everything was quiet in the van and Linda started to get up from their bed to pull out the air mattress. He intercepted her as she started to crawl over him and pulled her close. To his surprise Linda did not put up any resistance.

"She loves me," Malcolm decided. Her body relaxed as he kissed her firmly on the mouth and her body folded into his. Malcolm could feel his own body reacting as Linda deepened their kiss. Malcolm moved into a deeply penetrating kiss. Linda responded in kind. Malcolm moved his hand behind Linda's seat and started to massage her in sensual areas. He was amazed at Linda's response. Before long Malcolm was reaching to undo Linda's pajamas and slide them off her. He caressed her breasts and stomach with his mouth.

It was Linda that finally inserted Malcolm into her. She

moved on top of him and found a rhythm that made him gasp. He managed to withhold ejaculation long enough to satisfy Linda and then released himself with a passion that surprised himself. Linda withdrew and he cuddled her close. Her tears dropped onto his face to his surprise.

"If you only knew how long I've wanted you to do that," she told him as she held him close. Malcolm felt strange, warm vibrations around his heart.

"She needs me," he decided. It's been half a lifetime since I've felt like this," he said to himself in shock.

"I'm so sorry," Malcolm confessed. "I'm not a very good listener, am I?"

"No, you're not."

"I'll improve. I promise."

The next morning as Gus came out into the aisle of the motorhome Linda was still laying naked and entwined with Malcolm. Both their sets of pajamas were lying crumbled in the middle of the aisle. Gus smiled broadly as he took a closer look at both of his friends sleeping soundly.

"Finally," he said to Gloria as he retreated into the motorhome. "Finally we've got those two together."

"It's about time," Gloria responded, laughing loudly. "I was beginning to get a complex from Malcolm's continued rejection."

Gus got back into bed with Gloria.

"If we have to wait for them to wake up we might as well do it too," he laughed. "Good idea!" Gloria pulled her husband of many years firmly against her.

The motion of rocking shook the motorhome and the sound of chanting reached them from the bed above the driver's seat. Gloria realised that Tyler and Honey Pratt were having some kind of sex in the cab of the truck.

"That's everyone here, finally," she thought with a huge feeling of accomplishment. She wondered about Esther Goodenough and Art Malones. "The bet will have to be split at least four ways."

"You're an incorrigible matchmaker," Gus accused his wife as later they dressed for breakfast. "How many marriages are you responsible for now? I should make a movie about you."

CHAPTER 27.
Los Angeles.

Gus pulled into a large RV campsite just ahead of Los Angeles. He waited until Malcolm and Tyler had pulled the motor home and the other cargo truck into adjoining campsites and switched off his ignition. Everyone spilled out onto Gus's picnic table as Tyler went to pay the camping fee this time. No one noticed Norm Dixon pull into an empty campsite at the other end of the large lot. He had spotted the convoy from the air that morning, managed to catch up to it by noon with a powerful rental car, and followed just out of sight for the rest of the day.

"Too bad I can't see what's happening over there from here. I'll just have to wait till they all go to sleep," he decided. "And this time, I've got the solution to those cursed dogs."

Keith Dixon fondled his latest detective toy. It was a stun gun, designed to knock out humans without harming them. Keith lowered the charge by adjusting a setting. He thought about the fury of the Afro-American woman who owned the Pitbull when he had stepped on her dog's throat.

"Don't want to kill the little darlings, just put them to sleep for a while. Don't want that women coming at me again."

One hour later, as the distant lights of Los Angeles reflecting on the clouds illuminated the camp ground, Gus tied Bourbon to his usual position behind Tyler's truck with

Bea and Turk hidden inside. He tied Trump, this time, to the back of the truck he and Gloria were driving and allowed Cleo to enter the motor home to sleep beside Linda and Malcolm.

Norm Dixon waited until midnight to make his move.

"They'll all be asleep for sure by now," he thought.

The detective limped slowly but steadily through the park moving out of sight when any of the lights were on in the camping vehicles, positioned himself carefully above the parked convoy and glared at the Pitbull tied to the back door of one of the trucks. The dog looked like it had picked up his scent. It was growling and staring at him from the truck it was guarding. Norm placed the butt of the stun gun against his shoulder, fired the silent weapon and watched with a sense of satisfaction as the dog slumped to the ground, his red ball rolling out of his mouth as he hit the pavement.

"He'll be out for half an hour," the detective mused. Can't see that Doberman from here but I'll take care of her later if nothing is in this truck.

Norm moved confidently down to the back of Tyler's truck. Bourbon never moved. The detective smiled as he looked at the unconscious dog.

"Still breathing, I wouldn't want any trouble from his owner when she realises what I did to her dog."

Norm put down his stun gun. He moved to attack the padlock on the door with his bolt cutters. As he seized the padlock, a gust of wind moving in Trump's direction gave the already suspicious animal the scent of the large detective. The large Sheep Dog recognized the scent of his former adversary and went wild. He lunged as hard as he could and the leash attached to the back of the second vehicle snapped. The dog rushed in the direction of Norm Dixon's scent.

Norm dropped his bolt cutters as Trump's heavy breathing alerted him to his danger.

"God, it's not the Doberman," he thought as he turned and Trump knocked him to the ground. "Christ it's Malcolm Brook's Sheep Dog again." Sharp teeth bit into one of his arms as he desperately tried to crawl toward his stun gun. Norm's intense fear of dogs fired up even more and desperation gave him unusual strength. He managed to pull himself to his feet, dragged the sheep dog forward with his arm in its mouth, withstood the pain and grasped desperately at his stun gun. He fired the gun at Trump at close range with his one free arm and hand. The dog slumped to the ground next to Bourbon.

The detective's heart pounded fiercely as the lights in the motor home suddenly shot on.

"That damn dog and its barking!" Norm Dixon grabbed his stun gun and limped back to his car as fast as his heavy, damaged body would allow.

"Damn!" he cursed. As he reached his rental car Norm pulled the keys out of his pocket and jumped into the front seat. His arm as well as his foot and seat were burning from the dog bites. He sped out of the RV site and headed toward the freeway. Despair lit up the detective's heart.

"The Border," he muttered. "I'll have one more chance to intercept them at the Mexican Border. Maybe this time I'll use a real gun on those dogs."

Back at the campsite an anxious Linda Daniels was examining Bourbon and Trump as Gus and Tyler carried them into the motor home. They placed them on the table that Malcolm had recovered from him and Linda's bed. Honey Pratt looked on with great anxiety.

"I'm going to kill that cretin," she vowed.

"They're both breathing," Linda assured Honey and Malcolm.

"There are no marks on their bodies," she added.

"Likely used a stun gun," Malcolm figured out.

"The Bastard!" Honey exclaimed.

"You're likely right, Darling," Linda announced. "In that case they'll be all right. Should wake up in half an hour or so."

"We'll wait," Gus assured them.

"What about that intruder?"

"Won't be back anytime soon," Gus figured. "Likely that Detective again. Has to be sure Bea is with us before he notifies the authorities?"

"I'll kill him if he tries this again," Honey Pratt repeated, her arms around Bourbon.

"What about unconditional love?" Tyler reminded her.

"To Hell with unconditional love; should have killed the fat cretin the first time he stepped on Bourbon's throat."

Trump reached consciousness first. He whined anxiously and tried unsteadily to stand up. Malcolm grabbed him and held him tight. Linda noted that the man who was usually all business had tears of gratitude running down his face.

"Trump finally did something right for a change," Linda assured him. "His barks woke us and scared the fellow off."

Bourbon came back to consciousness several minutes later. He whined and then threw up all over the table. Linda quickly wiped up the mess and pressed a stethoscope to the dog's chest. Honey held him close and patted the weary Pit bull.

"I'll kill the bastard," Turk O'Brien vowed as Honey reported what had happened as an hour later as Tyler drove out of the RV park. Malcolm and Linda with Trump and Bourbon in the back bed followed in the motor home. Gus and Gloria were in the rear in the other cargo truck.

"He won't give up, I know he won't."

"We'll have to leave human sentries out tonight," Tyler

figured. "Bastard won't dare to use a stun gun on human beings."

"Hope you're right, Sugar."

Tyler pulled into an RV site just ahead of the Mexican Border later that night. Norm Dixon watched from the air with powerful binoculars as the convoy moved into the RV site.

"I'll intercept them in the morning," the determined detective vowed. "When they stop for Mexican insurance."

"Back to an airport?" inquired his pilot, now used to the detective's modus operandi.

Norm Dixon nodded.

"I'll check on what's in the back of the trucks when they go in for insurance tomorrow. It's my last chance."

"Good luck!"

"I'll keep watch," Tyler assured Gus and the others as they finished the meal that Gloria had managed. "I'll join you," Malcolm Brooks offered.

"Take Cleo with you, Darling."

"Too bad we don't have Dogzilla with us!" Honey muttered.

CHAPTER 28.
Mexican Border.

Close to dawn the next day Norm Dixon stood in nervous anticipation and considerable pain in a spot overlooking the cluster of Mexican insurance stores on the road to the Nogales Border crossing. His rear end was now too sore to sit for long on it. He was afraid it was infected again.

"They'll all have to go in to get Mexican insurance before they go over the border," he plotted to himself. "I'll follow and make my move when they go to buy it. I have to be certain Bea Broughton is with them before I contact U.S. border guards."

An hour later he spotted the convoy as it made its way to the border. The three vehicles pulled into the Mexican Insurance Sales parking lot just as he had expected. The detective pulled in just close enough to keep a watch on the occupants. He waited until they were safely into the store, picked up his stun gun and drew a package of raw meat out of the passenger side.

"Damn, they've left the dogs inside this time! But at least it's so early there's no one in the lot."

Norm headed to the cargo truck driven by Tyler Thompson. He frowned as he encountered the large padlock that Tyler had fastened to the back door. The detective quickly pulled a pair of bolt cutters out of his pocket and attacked the padlock.

Inferno started barking from inside the truck. Bea and Turk quickly moved into their places inside the coffins. Bourbon sniffed the air, detected the scent of his tormentor from the other times and started growling fiercely. Turk did not pull his lock down as Tyler had told him to do.

"Anyone that pulls this coffin open is going to get a surprise," he vowed. He pulled out the gun he had managed to obtain when Gus had stopped in the Walmart parking lot.

Norm Dixon flung the destroyed padlock to the side and pulled up the back door of the truck. Inferno and Bourbon came running at him and he threw the dogs both a chunk of raw meat. The dogs grabbed the meat and sat down on the floor to eat it. Norm quickly fired his stun gun at both the dogs. They slumped onto the floor. Norm's elation that his plan had worked turned to great disappointment as he glanced around the inside of the truck.

"Just coffins," he cursed. Then a couple of objects suddenly caught his eye. There were two empty coffee cups sitting in one of the corners of the truck.

"They're here," he muttered to himself. He pulled at the lid of one of the top coffins but it was locked.

"Damn." Norm reached for his bolt cutters again but he did not get the chance to use them. Bourbon was not completely unconscious. The dog shook his head trying desperately to get to his feet. The unsteady dog managed to reach the detective's right foot and seized it again. Norm screamed in pain as Bourbon reopened the wound. He tried to shake the enraged animal off but the dog pulled him toward the open door of the truck.

"No," he screamed as Bourbon bit even more deeply into his heel. The detective frantically threw his body toward the door. One more agonized push and both him and Bourbon crashed out the door and onto the pavement. Norm's large body hit the concrete with considerable force and his pain was intense. He desperately tried to dislodge Bourbon. Norm screamed as the Pitbull seemed to regain more of his strength and started to drag him across the parking lot.

Inside the truck, the top of a coffin suddenly flew open and Turk O'Brien leaped out. He jumped out of the truck, took one look and realised that the Detective was trying desperately to pull his revolver out of its holster with his one unbitten arm. He started to aim his own gun but thought better of it and hurled himself at the Detective. Before the gun in the holster could be pulled out and fired a sharp right from the enraged, former racing car driver connected solidly to the detective's jaw and knocked him unconscious. Norm Dixon lay ominously still on the ground.

Turk looked around. Miraculously there was still no one was in the parking lot and there was no one responding to the noise from the Insurance office. Turk thanked God that Tyler had parked so far away from the office.

"Let go Bourbon," he ordered, patting the dog and massaging him on his back.

"Good dog!" Bourbon spit out the detective's bleeding foot. Turk picked up the unconscious detective and staggered with the weight of the heavy fellow. He made it into the back of Tyler's truck. He whistled for Bourbon and the dog staggered in. Turk checked out Tyler's unconscious dog in the dog bed.

"He's still breathing, no thanks to that fellow."

Turk glanced out the rear door of the truck. Still, no one seemed to be watching. He put the door down and then reached for a package of tape from Tyler's tool box and taped the detective's mouth. He secured his arms to his sides and tied up his legs. He ignored the blood seeping from the detective's foot. Turk lifted off the coffin he was supposed to be in and pulled open the door of the coffin below. He pulled a sharp screw driver from Tyler's tool box, forced a couple of holes in the coffin using his unusual strength and heaved the still unconscious detective's large bulk into it. He wound the sticky, plastic tape around and around the man. Norm Dixon now resembled an Egyptian mummy. Turk closed the top of the coffin.

"No way he's going to kick or bang with that around him," he decided.

"What's going on," Bea shouted through her coffin.

"Don't worry Sweetheart," Turk assured her. "It's that detective again. But Bourbon took care of the problem this time." He glanced at the Pit

bull who was looking rather unsteady but was still conscious.

"Must have developed a resistance to the stun gun," he figured. "Those Pitbulls are tough all right."

Turk picked up the detective's stun gun lying on the floor, removed the pistol out of his holder, put down the lid on the detective's coffin and climbed back into his own coffin taking the weapons along.

Twenty minutes later Tyler and the others came back to the vehicles and him, Malcolm and Gus moved into their driver's seats. No one spotted the missing lock on the cargo truck. Tyler moved out onto the road that led to the lineup for the border crossing and the others followed.

At the border the guard recognized Tyler who had made the trip across at Nogales many times. He did little but a cursory check of the ownership and insurance papers for both of Tyler's trucks, issued a one hundred, eighty-day permit, looked at everyone's passport and motioned he and Malcolm through.

The guard was a little more thorough with Gus's ownership and insurance papers but made no attempt to inspect the inside of the vehicle. The convoy moved forward into Mexico.

About twelve miles later they were stopped again at the vehicle inspection station. Their permits and their Mexican insurance papers were examined and the guard requested that Tyler open the back doors of the two cargo trucks. Tyler freaked at the missing lock on his truck but said nothing. He opened the back and patted Inferno, who was now awake, and Bourbon as they came toward him. The animals gave no sign that anything was wrong and obeyed Tyler as he ordered them to sit. Tyler held his breath but the guards just stared at the coffins and then motioned him to close the door of the truck. The guards moved to Malcolm's truck but when the truck was opened one of the guards went inside and pulled up the lids of the top coffins. Seeing nothing he abandoned the search.

At Gus's motorhome the guards searched through the suitcases and had a look at the inside of the fridge and food cupboards. Then they nodded and indicated that the convoy was free to move on.

Tyler pulled out onto the road, followed by Malcolm and Gus and headed for his destination at Guadalajara. He barely got underway and there was a tapping noise on the window. Honey Pratt opened it and started at the expression on Turk O'Brien's face.

"What's the problem, Sugar?"

"You'll have to pull off the road, Tyler."

"Whatever for?"

"I'll show you. Make sure you pull off somewhere where there's no one to see us."

About twenty minutes later Tyler moved onto a dirt road heading out into the desert and drove along it for a few miles. He waited until Gus and Malcolm had pulled their rigs off the road and then went around to the back of the truck and lifted the door. The dogs greeted him joyously and Turk helped Bea out of the truck. He motioned the men to follow him inside.

Turk brought Gus, Tyler and Malcolm up to the top coffin on the right and opened it.

"Christ," Gus exclaimed. Malcolm gasped as they stared at what now looked like a large Egyptian mummy.

"What the Hell is he doing in there?"

"Bastard cut the lock off the back door when you guys went for insurance. Found him being chewed up by Bourbon and put him to sleep for a while."

The figure wrapped in the duct taped struggled to free itself and made choking noises from behind all the tape. Turk slammed the coffin shut.

"Better take off that tape around his mouth," Malcolm suggested. "He could choke if he throws up or something." Turk ignored him.

"Bastard shot the dogs with that stun gun again. Lucky Bourbon must have built up some resistance to the charge or maybe it was just sheer will power on his part!"

"Where is the stun gun?"

Turk pulled the weapon out of his coffin along with his own and the gun belonging to the detective.

"You took those over the border! We would have been put in the slammer for years if the border guards had found them."

"Give me the guns!" Tyler ordered.

Turk handed the guns to Tyler. Tyler took out a hammer from his tool chest and in a series of blows rendered the guns useless. He wiped his finger prints from them and tossed them out into the desert behind a cactus tree.

Gus motioned the men out of the truck and far enough away that the detective could not hear them.

"What the Hell do we do now?"

"Leave him in the desert with the guns."

"We can't do that Turk! He might die out here."

The ladies came over and joined the men.

"Bea's told us what happened."

Malcolm Brooks suddenly took charge. He told the group that he would go and try and reason with the detective.

"Better take Turk with you," Tyler advised. "That fellow may not be in a reasoning mood."

Malcolm and Turk moved back inside the truck. Malcolm raised the lid of the coffin and told the detective to calm down, that they were going to let him out if he behaved himself. Muffled sounds were all they could make out. Malcolm reached for the tape around the fellow's mouth and pulled it off.

"I'll put you all in a Mexican jail forever," the large detective threatened.

"Quiet down," Turk ordered. He grabbed the detective around his throat.

"Let's be reasonable," Malcolm pleaded. "Or do you want us to drive off and leave you here with Turk?"

The detective looked at Turk O'Brien and the wild look in his eye.

"All right, it's a deal," he muttered.

Malcolm unwrapped the tape from around the detective and him and Turk pulled the fellow out of the coffin.

"Have a seat!" Malcolm motioned the detective to have a seat on Inferno's dog bed. The detective collapsed on the bed. He groaned as Malcolm looked at his foot, pulled a handkerchief from his pocket and tried to stop the seeping of blood from his foot.

"Turk, you go and get Linda and the first aid kit out of the motorhome," Malcolm ordered.

"Shout if he does anything." Turk moved to the outside of the truck.

Malcolm asked the detective what it was going to take to make him forget what had happened.

"All we want is for you to look the other way." Malcolm's words seemed to throw the detective into a rage.

"Ain't never taken a bribe, never in my life."

The fellow's attitude infuriated Malcolm. He gave him a lecture about how unjust it was of Bea's son to have put her into the care home in the first place. He told the detective that there was absolutely nothing wrong with Bea's mind and that his team of lawyers would immediately notify the police where she was and seek to invalidate the "Power of Attorney" now that she was safe from being forcibly returned to the care home.

"Talk to Bea yourself. You'll see that her mind is perfectly intact. That's the least you can do. Look at all the trouble you've caused!"

Malcolm's lecture seemed to make an impact on the detective.

"My mother wound up in one of those places," he confided.

"Then you'll have a chat?"

Norm Dixon nodded and Malcolm moved toward the rear door of the truck. The detective managed to stand up, limped after him unsteadily and Malcolm helped him down to the road. He went over to the ladies and introduced Bea to the detective. Tyler restrained Honey as she glared at the detective.

"What's your name?" Bea asked politely.

Norm Dixon introduced himself and Bea suggested they go into the motorhome and get some bandages and water.

"Not without me," Turk O'Brien insisted.

The detective nodded and all three of them plus Linda went into the motorhome. The others waited anxiously in the shade of one of the trucks. Linda used her medical kit to bandage up and disinfect Norm Dixon's foot and other wounds. She had to make a series of stitches to close up the wounds.

"It will be all right," she assured him. "No permanent damages or scarring."

Thirty minutes later Norm Dixon said goodbye to his one hundred thousand dollars, his reputation and his licence. He could tell that Bea Broughton's mind was in better shape than his own. He held out his hand to her.

"Thought there was something funny about this case. It's obvious that you shouldn't be in a care home."

"Then you'll let us proceed to Guadalajara?"

"Sure but you might as well let me stay here in Mexico, I'll have to tell John Broughton what happened and where his mother is now. My detective's license will be revoked. I'm sure of it. Not to mention all the expenses I've run up."

"I'll cover your expenses," Turk O'Brien advised. "We'll drop you at the next large town. One with a car rental agency."

"Right, I won't have been in Mexico for more than seventy-two hours. They'll probably just let me go back. I've got my passport with me."

All four went outside and Turk told the others that they had reached an agreement. Everyone sighed with relief. Shortly afterward the convoy moved back onto the highway with Norm Dixon riding with Malcolm and Linda in the motor home. Trump was in the back with Cleo for a change. Malcolm decided to sweeten the deal with Norm Dixon in case he had second thoughts.

"You know, Norm, I like the way you acted on your hunch and tracked us down."

"Happens all the time. I seem to know somehow what people are up to."

"I'm looking for a Chief of Security for my race horse installations. I suspect one of my employees doped my race horse, Starwalker, before the Kentucky Derby. Think you might be interested?"

"Where would the job be located?"

"Kentucky mainly. But I have facilities in three states. You'd have to travel every so often."

"I've been wanting to move into something else."

"Great. Have you got a business card?"

Norm Dixon pulled out a card from his wallet. Malcolm told him he would get a call from his personnel office. A short time later the convoy stopped in Hemosillo and Tyler negotiated a rental car for the detective. He spoke perfect Spanish. Malcolm got Tyler to get through to his office on the phone, told them that Bea was now in Mexico and gave instructions to his lawyers to proceed with the plan for revoking Bea Broughton's Power of Attorney. He also phoned and instructed his Personnel Chief to get in touch with Norm Dixon about making him the Head of Security for his racing stables.

"Create the position and make it for one hundred forty thousand a year."

Linda smiled as she heard Malcolm's order.

"You handed that masterfully," she congratulated Malcolm as he hung up the phone. Malcolm beamed.

"It shouldn't be long," Malcolm put his arm around Bea Broughton. "My lawyers say three weeks at the most and it should be possible for you to return."

"I'll call John and try and get him to see reason."

Malcolm shook his head.

"Let my lawyers handle the matter for now. As soon as they give the go ahead, you can contact your son."

Bea's eyes filled with tears but she nodded.

"Just long enough for a Mexican vacation," Gus stated. "How about we all go to Puerto Vallarta after we drop off Tyler's coffins?"

"Why not?" Tyler seconded the motion. Honey Pratt laughed.

"Another three weeks. Charlotte is going to have a nervous breakdown."

"Why don't we take advantage and conduct a couple of Mexican weddings while we're at it?" He looked Honey Pratt straight in the eye. She felt massive warm vibrations around her heart as she realised he was asking her to marry him. Honey never hesitated.

"Think y'all is the love of my life, Sugar."

Tyler kissed her passionately. She responded in kind.

"Uh, Linda, I know I don't deserve you but would you consider marrying me?" Malcolm Brooks eyed Linda with pleading in his eyes.

"You want a permanent caretaker for your animals?"

"I deserve that! No, I want a permanent playmate."

"What about your baby, Malcolm, when it's born?"

"You'll make a good stepmother."

Linda broke into a beaming smile and tears ran down her eyes. Malcolm seized her and they embraced for a long time.

"Turk and I would like to get married too!" Bea informed the others.

Turk smiled and nodded. He pulled Bea against him.

"Maybe we should renew our vows," Gus suggested to Gloria.

"Of course, Darling! What a good idea."

"We'll stop in Mazatland and pick up some rings," Tyler decided.

"I'll phone Art, Esther, Virgie and Frank. Maybe they'll come down and join us too," Gloria volunteered.

"And our dogs," Turk ordered. "They can have them flown down."

"Better let me phone Charlotte and I'll ask her to come down," Honey Pratt sighed. "That girl is going to think I had a personality fracture for sure. Marrying at such a late date in life. She and Tyler need to get to know each other."

CHAPTER 29.
Guadalajara.

Turk O'Brien wandered the streets of Guadalajara with his arm wound around Bea Broughton. Great joy was in his heart. He could not believe that they had made it safely to their destination. Turk was letting the atmosphere of Guadalajara soak into his being. Mexican music was everywhere. Senoritas dressed in colourful costumes reaching down to the ground strolled the streets. Musicians wearing tall sombreros and fancy Mexican dress outfits played guitars, trumpets and mariachi's almost on every street corner. Pillars from Colonial architecture dating as far back as the seventeenth century reached up to touch the sky everywhere.

Turk stopped at one of the portable stands selling Tamales and bought two. He handed Bea one of them and they sat on one of the many benches in front of one of the old churches to watch the busy street life go by.

"I'm going to phone John," Turk shook his head in shock as Bea's voice was filled with determination.

"Malcolm said to wait until his lawyers give the go-ahead."

"By that time we could already be married, Dear. I want to give John, Orphelia and the children time to get down here to join us."

Turk's euphoric mood vanished. He was afraid that Bea was setting herself up for another bitter disappointment.

"Well, I guess that detective fellow's been in contact by this time. Watch out for Orphelia if she answers the phone, though."

"I'll hang up if that's the case."

Turk handed Bea his cell phone.

"Melissa, it's Granny, how are you."

Turk realised that Bea's oldest granddaughter had answered the phone. He noted that Bea had tears in her eyes. He noticed her expression change to apprehension and figured that he son or daughter-in-law had picked up the phone.

"No, I'm certainly not coming back any time soon," Bea yelled in anger. "Let me speak to my son!"

Turk listened as Bea had a highly charged emotion session with her son on the phone. After several minutes Bea broke into tears again. He handed her a handkerchief as he could see she was desperately trying to withhold her tears. He felt proud as she managed to issue an ultimatum to John Broughton.

"I want you to come to the wedding, John. It's going to be in Puerto Vallarta. I'll mail the tickets. Come to the wedding and I'll make some financial arrangements in favour of you and Orphelia. But I'll not make a move to stop the termination of that Power of Attorney."

Turk sighed as Bea abruptly closed the cell phone.

"I'll give them the house," she told Turk with tears in her eyes. "But I'll not give up you for anything."

Turk drew her close to him and they embraced.

"I have a feeling that at least your son and granddaughters will come down, Bea."

"I hope so."

In another corner of Guadalajara Tyler Thompson laughed at the expression on his face as one of his Mexican partners questioned the condition of the coffin that the detective had been resting in.

"Don't worry my friend, that coffin's a write off. We'll deduct it from the invoice."

Honey Pratt groaned as she put down the telephone after having one of her perplexing conversations with her daughter Charlotte and admired her fiancee's capacity for unconditional love and compassion. He had lost money on the latest shipment of coffins, not to mention the extra expense of hauling his friends down to Mexico but only cared about helping his fellow member of the Dog Walking Club.

"Such a difference from my usual suitors," Honey thought with a smile. "They're usually hitting on me for money to buy the latest flashy sports car or technological toy."

"Is Charlotte coming to the wedding?" Tyler asked as they went out of the Mexican funeral home hand-in-hand.

Honey groaned as she thought about her upsetting conversation with her youngest offspring.

"She's in hysterics, Sugar. She's convinced I'm doing something I will regret for the rest of my life."

"And are you?" Honey could feel Tyler's intense look probing right into her sixth centre.

"Y'all are the best thing that ever happened to me, Sugar." Honey promised.

Tyler kissed her passionately in front of all the passerbys on the busy street.

"We'll send her tickets anyway."

"Three sets, Sugar. She's bringing my two grown-up sons and their wives down too. To convince me I'm ruining my life."

They laughed and embraced again.

"Crazy tourists!" could be heard from observers. Tyler and Honey were blissfully unaware of their stares and giggles.

On another phone in one of the charming Period hotels of Guadalajara Gloria was on the phone with Art and Esther.

"We're coming," Gloria smiled as Esther advised her that she and Art would send the dogs down right away and come themselves.

"Virgie and Frank are coming as well as their dogs. Make sure you make the marriage arrangements for all four of us, too."

Gloria made sure she was getting the message straight.

"Virgie and Frank and their dogs. You're sure?"

Gloria went into peals of laughter as Esther told her that they had no choice. She told Gloria about Tyler's housekeeper coming into their bedroom in the midst of one of their heavy sex sessions. Esther added that the housekeeper belonged to the same church and had gone straight to their minister. The minister had told them to marry immediately or face the eternal fires of Hell. Esther said that they were only too happy to oblige.

CHAPTER 30.
Puerto Vallarta Area.

The rays of the sunset lit up the terrace of the ancient temple as Linda Daniels, sitting next to Malcolm Brooks on the terraced stairs of the Aztec temple, stared at the twelve dogs sitting shoulder to shoulder on one of the wide stairs.

"Look at the dogs, Darling. They look like they're watching the ceremony."

Malcolm Brooks stared at the dogs. Trump, Cleo, Inuvik, Gigi, Bourbon, Dante, Dogzilla, Lazarus, Angus, Mozart, Bookkeeper and Pegasus sat perfectly still on the terraced stairs in front of them. It looked like they were staring at the Mexican Judge who was marrying Honey Pratt and Tyler Thompson.

"They likely are watching, my dear. They understand more than we think. I'll try and get a shot of them before it's our turn."

Linda watched the man she was about to marry scamper up the terraced stairs high enough to get all the dogs in a panoramic shot. She stared at the myriads of flaming torches down below that lit up the wedding reception area on the white, sand beach that could only be accessed by water and listened to the Mexican mariachi, trumpet and guitar music drifting up to the marriage participants and their guests under the old temple site.

Linda recalled her deep emotions that morning as all of the participants in Gloria's bet had indulged in a purification ceremony in the hot tub at the luxurious spa overlooking the ocean.

"Ten years I've loved Malcolm from afar and now we'll spend whatever time we have left together." Her emotions had deepened as she thought of Monica's child. "And I'm to be a stepmother." All reports had Monica proceeding well with the pregnancy. "This must be Heaven and I've reached it somehow."

Linda felt tears run down her face as Honey and Tyler were pronounced "Man and Wife." They stood up from their kneeling position near the cliff's edge under a white canopy, before a white altar, and embraced passionately. Linda noticed Malcolm snap a shot of Honey's daughter Charlotte as she wiped a tear from her eye. Honey's two sons and their wives were standing next to Charlotte. They had smiles on their faces.

"Charlotte and Tyler must have finally hit it off," Linda laughed as she remembered how Tyler had turned his considerable charm on for Honey's three offspring when they had arrived from the mainland. "And they came to try and stop the wedding." Charlotte had convinced the others that her mother had suffered a personality fracture.

Linda glanced around her at her other friends sitting around her waiting for their ceremonies. Honey and Tyler moved into the seated area and Virginia Kelly and Frank Simpson kneeled before the Judge.

Linda watched as Malcolm snapped a shot of Virgie and Frank, their grown up children and then finally sat down on the stairs far enough behind the dogs to get another panorama camera shot of their backs.

"He's got the picture," she thought. "What an incredible shot! Looks like someone spend hours positioning the dogs." Malcolm's flash lit up the area as he took several pictures of the animals. Then Linda reeled as she spotted the parrots flying toward the palm tree only ten feet from the dogs.

"Oh no," Linda watched in horror as Trump broke formation first and leaped off the terrace steps to create havoc. The local, wild, red and green parrots were flying in and reaching their nesting spot for the night. Raucous screams echoed throughout the air and drowned out Virginia and Frank saying their vows. Squaring parrots berated the large Sheep Dog and then four of his friends as they joined him to interfere with their night rituals. Linda broke into laughter as Dogzilla particularly seemed to be trying to knock the solid palm tree down. The dog hurled his bulk against the tree's trunk again and again. As Malcolm watched and captured the scene with photos, Linda could see that coconuts were being shaken out of the tree and were hurtling down on top of Pegasus, Inferno, and Inuvik. Little Lazarus was barking furiously from his perch on the terrace stairs at the antics of his large friends. Cleo sat obediently as she had been told to do. Mozart and Angus seemed confused by all the noise, and Bookkeeper and Bourbon faithfully stared down at the wedding ceremony.

The command "Freeze," reached Linda as Turk O'Brien's powerful voice ordered his errant dog to cease his wedding disturbance antics. The large Rottweiler immediately sank to the ground. Linda groaned as Malcolm yelled "Down" at Trump and the stubborn Sheep Dog ignored him completely as usual.

"That dog!" Linda sighed. "He continues to be a crime wave on four legs. I'm going to have to get Malcolm to be more authoritarian with him."

As Linda watched, Trump was still leaping up at the remaining parrots in the trees. Then Linda nodded in approval as Malcolm suddenly seemed to realise he had the remote to Trump's radio collar in the pocket of his formal, white suit and pressed the warning buzzer. As Linda took in the scene Trump turned to stare at Malcolm as if to ask if he really meant it. Malcolm pointed back onto the steps and the dog returned to his position next to Cleo with his tail dragging between his legs. Pegasus and Inferno were now alone at the Palm tree and they stared longingly at their friends lined up again on the terrace steps. Without their leader, Trump, they seemed dispirited. Both dogs slowly moved to the other side of Cleo. Lazarus finally stopped his frantic barking and the Mexican judge's voice could be heard again up in the stands.

"Until death do you part."

"Well that's very final." Linda vagariously enjoyed Virginia's and Frank's spirited embrace as the second ceremony ended.

"Imagine what they are going to do on their honeymoon," Linda sighed. Virgie had been confiding their interest in far out sex practices to her friends in the spa that morning.

Linda watched as Bea Broughton and Turk O'Brien moved into kneeling positions in front of the judge and Malcolm focused his camera on John Broughton and Bea's two grandchildren. The flash exploded as he snapped a quick shot of the trio.

"Nice that John and the children flew down after that call from Bea even if he was the cause of all that trouble. Too bad that Orphelia refused to join them, though."

When Malcolm rejoined Linda they both now focused on Art Maloney and Esther Goodenough saying their wedding vows. The older couple embraced joyfully as their ceremony ended and Linda felt warmth surge through her heart as Malcolm seized her hand tenderly and he led her down to the altar. It was their turn to marry.

"Thank God it's you I've married," Linda's heart throbbed as Malcolm whispered to her following the end of the ceremony. It seemed forever as he kissed her sensuously. She could feel his affection strongly as he held her against him. Malcolm led her back to the stairs and they watched Gloria and Gus Gustafson take their places for the Vow Renewal.

"I can't believe Virginia and Frank!" Malcolm whispered. "Who would have thought people their age were going to spend their honeymoon learning Scuba Diving and then diving with the sharks off Mazatland?"

"I'm worried about them. Do you suppose they're developing an obsession for Adrenaline?"

"Could be. But what about Honey and Tyler going off communing in the open ocean with the dolphins from a catamaran?"

Linda laughed. "Fits Honey to a 'T'."

"Hope Trump sits still in that Cessna as we head out to stay in the authentic Aztec village in the mountains."

"Make sure you bring along that radio collar and the remote."

"Good idea."

"Art and Esther are the only sensible ones amongst us," Linda sighed. "They're heading back to Guadalajara for a tour of the Tequila factory and the shopping centres."

"What about Turk and Bea?"

"He's taking her to the Bull fights."

"Yuk!"

She noticed Malcolm relax as she told him that the bulls were never killed in Mexico.

"He's so attuned to animals, just like me."

"What about Gloria and Gus?" Linda asked as they knelt in their places before the Mexican judge. Malcolm put a finger to his lips as the judge began the vow renewal ceremony. Linda had to wait until after Gus's fervent embrace of his wife at the end of the ceremony to find out where they were going. As the crowd moved down the trail to the torches and the gayly decorated tables for the reception, Malcolm told her that Gus and Gloria would be joining an adventurous group taking on the rigours of a hiking and cliff climbing experience near the wedding site.

"These cliffs?"

"Yes, after they take part in a forest canopy excursion in the rain forest further down the coast."

"Forest canopies excursion?"

"You know, using platforms and ropes to surge through the tops of the trees."

"Like Tarzan?"

"Of course!" Linda cringed as Malcolm let out a Tarzan imitation yell as startled friends congratulated them on their wedding.

"What about Gigi and Inuvik?"

"They're going along. Gus paid for them, too. I wish I could see the dogs thrashing through the jungle trying to keep up with Gus and Gloria in the trees. Maybe we should join them with Trump and Cleo?"

"With Trump? He'd take off chasing feral pigs or some other exotic animal for sure."

Linda laughed as she could see the sudden gleam in Malcolm's eyes.

"Let's do it. There's still space on the estate near Gus and Gloria's house for more animals. We can do the Cessna trip after."

"You're incorrigible. Monica might want to visit her child, you know. You'll freak her out again."

"I've always wanted a wild pig for my collection."

239945

Made in the USA